Leopold Hamilton Myers was born in Cambridge in 1881. Both his grandfather and great-grandfather were writers and his father was a well-known man of letters. After Eton and Trinity College, Cambridge, he became a temporary clerk in the Foreign Office and remained there for the duration of the First World War. In 1921 he published his first novel *The Orissers*. He died in 1944.

(AUNT)
LADY OSWESTRY (MARION)
JANE
MARIE
HUGO
HARRY
ANGELA PAUNCEFORT
MARY WESTONBURY — GERALD
LADY OLGA SWINTON
DOCTOR McCLAREN
HUGH STANFORD
CAPTAIN WILSON
VEEDER
TOMMY SIMPSON
SIR JAMES ANNESLEY
STELLA BARBON — JOCK
FRANCES TILLING
SCHMIDT
PROF. BROWN
APPLEBY WILKINSON
SEÑOR JOAO DA PINTA CUNHA
JOACHIM (HIS SON)

The
Clio

by L. H. Myers

Robin Clark
London

First published in paperback by Robin Clark in 1990
27/29 Goodge Street
London W1P 1FD

First published by G.P. Putnam's Sons, Ltd in 1925
© L.H. Myers 1925

This book is sold subject to the condition that it shall not, by way of trade or otherwise, be lent, sold, hired out, or otherwise circulated without the Publisher's prior consent in any form of binding or cover other than that in which it is published and without a similar condition including this condition being imposed on the subsequent purchaser. This book is published at a net price and is supplied subject to the Publishers Association Standard Conditions of Sale registered under the Restrictive Trades Practices Act 1956.

British Library Cataloguing in Publication Data
Myers, L.H. (Leopold Hamilton), 1881–1944
The Clio.
I. Title
823'.912[F]
ISBN 0-86072-125-6

**Printed and bound in Great Britain by
Cox & Wyman Ltd., Reading, Berks.**

Chapter 1

THE *Clio*, probably the most expensive steam-yacht in the world, was cleaving a sea of glass. In a pearly-blue sky the sun made a white blot of furious heat. Each part of the circular horizon was exactly similar to every other part. It was a scene of peace.

The *Clio* was white and gleaming. So clean was she, so freshly painted, so well-groomed, so arrogant, that one felt she must have come straight from the hands of a beauty specialist. And she was young. She had been launched only five years ago.

The caprice of her mistress, Lady Oswestry, was now speeding her down the forty-eighth western parallel of longitude, which she decorated with a frothy wake and an occasional empty bottle. Her latitude at 9 a.m. on November 5th in the year 1925 (the moment at which this tale opens) was 3° 2′ 26″ North—from which the reader will perceive that she was not very far from the mouth of the Amazon.

Lady Oswestry had been a widow for some years —exactly how many the inconspicuous character of her husband made it difficult to remember. Her friends, whilst admitting that her looks suggested forty, computed that fifty-one was her probable age. She was tall, broad-shouldered, straight-backed, with slim ankles and well-shaped hands and feet. Her eyes were green, her hair copious and richly brown, her nose and mouth were perfect.

Every morning at nine o'clock she took a bath in the yellow marble bathroom adjoining her large, pale, perfumed cabin. The glass jars of bath salts on the shelf made sequences of colour which she stared at with pleasure from the cool water. This morning the sequence happened to be mauve, white, green (Suffragette, she reflected with a contemptuous smile), pink, white, purple, yellow, white, green, and orange. After her bath she went through her physical exercises and then returned to her cabin ready for the great task of the day.

She kept two maids. The first, Jane, attended to her person; the second, Marie, to her clothes. Jane was standing by the big glass-topped dressing-table. Spread out in readiness for her ladyship was an astonishingly various and intricate toilet equipment. Lady Oswestry seated herself, took up a hand-mirror, and examined her face. Her scrutiny lasted for nearly ten minutes.

Jane was an Englishwoman of middle-age, tall, stern-featured, dark. She scorned to wear anything but black, even in the tropics. Her sombre figure was conspicuous in the pale room where shades of aquamarine predominated. The light that filtered through the slatted shutters gave a strong, even illumination; the cabin was dim only by contrast with the few white-hot needles of light that darted in between shutter and window-frame. Some of them struck and splintered upon the crystal, steel, and silver with which the dressing-table was strewn. They reminded you that the world outside was white and blazing. They made the silent, coolly-tinted cabin seem like an aquarium tank, in which mistress and maid were a silver and a dark-hued fish. Into this aquamarine, aqueous interior there penetrated distantly the hum of the ship's engines, the swish of the cloven sea, and occasionally the murmur of a voice.

Without a sigh Lady Oswestry put down her mirror and started operations. Her expression, habitually careless and audacious, was now stern. Jane hovered, attentive. Her business was to proffer the right thing at the right moment. And this she did unfailingly.

About two hours later it was Marie's turn. The girl came in carrying the clothes which her mistress was to wear. Lady Oswestry took ten minutes to put her things on, and was about to leave the room when Hugo, her younger son, lounged in. He sat himself on the foot of the bed, and after mopping his flushed face, exhibited the handkerchief soaked through with perspiration.

"I'm hot," said he.

"My darling, I do wish you wouldn't! You'll get sunstroke or heat apoplexy."

Hugo was a beautiful youth of twenty-three—red-brown hair, blue eyes, white skin. Of medium height and slim, he carried his clothes to perfection. At this moment, however, he was wearing nothing but a shirt and trousers of the thinnest tussore.

"Marie, get me a glass of soda-water, will you?"

Marie, who was gazing at him in rapt admiration, ran off. His mother pushed his moist hair back from his brow and, after carefully drying a little patch of forehead with her handkerchief, bent down and kissed it.

"My precious, my beautiful Hugo! I'm afraid that girl's in love with you. Of course, all women are. How can they help it!"

"How, indeed?" returned Hugo composedly. "I've punched that ball for an hour and a quarter altogether," he went on, "giving it about eighty a minute."

"It seems such a silly thing to do," said Lady Oswestry. "But if it keeps you fit. . . ."

"It does. Besides, I've got to box Toby Travers the moment we get back to London. It's a bet. Thank you, Marie," he added, taking a long, full glass from the girl's hand.

Through the open door Lady Oswestry caught sight of someone passing. "Is that you, James?" she called.

A charming but weary male voice, the voice of an oldish man, answered her. At once she went out.

Marie, golden-haired, short-skirted, very much the soubrette, began tripping about the room, stooping down to show off ankles and calves, reaching up in order to display bust and arms. Hugo sipped his soda-water, supremely unconcerned.

"Ah! mais, monsieur, ce matin il fait une chaleur!" And she lifted her hands.

Hugo shrugged. "Oh, pas tant que ça."

"Est-ce-que monsieur——" She stopped with a slightly exaggerated start. A tall, dark, scowling figure had appeared upon the threshold.

"Hullo, Harry!" said Hugo.

His elder brother grunted.

"Seen the captain? Are we likely to get into Para to-night?"

Harry paid no attention to these questions. "If you think punching that ball—is going to make a boxer of you——" He finished his sentence with a laugh. "I'll take you on any day—with one hand."

He spoke in jerks. The sound of his deep mumbling voice was followed by a silence during which Marie could not forbear to flash an indignant look over her shoulder.

"No, thanks," said Hugo with a slightly forced smile. "I'd sooner take on Carpentier."

It had been on the tip of his tongue to say "a gorilla." For although tall, well-made, and giving an impression of elegance, Harry was, in some ways, rather like one. The forward hang of his shoulders and his long arms were responsible. Moreover, he had a heavy, protruding jaw and a forehead that receded. Its backward slope was accentuated by his fashion of wearing his hair. It was combed straight away from the forehead and plastered, jet-black and glistening, down on to the scalp.

Harry said no more, but continued to stand in the doorway. His eyes, the irises of which were singularly dark, moved this way and that, and his nostrils twitched as he sniffed the air. Marie had been cooling it with scented spray from a large atomizer. Its freshness and fragrance evidently pleased him. He smiled, showing his teeth, and advanced while Marie rather ostentatiously retreated. His grin became fixed, he followed and headed her round towards the door, then——

"Shoo!" said he, throwing up his arms as though chasing out a chicken. Marie fled.

Hugo put down his glass and rose. "I must have a bath."

"The water's yellow and brackish," said Harry.

"How's that?" asked Hugo. Then he bethought himself. "Oh, yes! We're getting into Amazon water. Land in sight yet?"

"No."

Hugo looked at the floor. "I should like to know"—then he hesitated—"what you want to do—up the Amazon."

Harry gave a chuckle. "It'll amuse me considerably—to see the young women's complexions—after the insects have had a go at them." He paused. "You'll know which you really love best—end of this trip, Hugo, me lad."

Hitching up his too well-creased trousers, he seated himself on the sofa. His movements were deliberate and marked by a sort of heavy swagger. Hands on knees, he stuck out his elbows and eyed his younger brother with kindly contemptuousness. He looked as if he were going to say something. But Hugo did not wait.

With half-closed eyes Harry sat there. His nostrils expanded as he inhaled the scented atmosphere. He stretched out a long arm, picked up a bottle of perfume, and sniffed it, but without taking out the stopper. The sound of girls' voices and a burst of laughter came from a cabin somewhere forward. He got up, and whilst surveying himself in the mirror practised first an expression of princely blandness and then a particularly ferocious scowl.

Lounging down the passage, he stopped upon reaching the doctor's door. It was open, and on the settee opposite sat three girls side by side. Although their appearance bespoke them young ladies of fashion, it was evident that they had "got the giggles" and were indulging themselves to the top of their bent.

The first, Angela Pauncefort, was twenty-two years of age—*une blonde cendrée*, with a pretty, aristocratic, but insignificant face. She was dressed in a hand-blocked tunic-frock, her pale mauve stockings matching the pattern on the dress. Next to her was Mary Westonbury, nineteen, small, slender, with pale olive skin and dark brown hair. She wore white crêpe-de-Chine with a dark blue scarf which fell over the right shoulder. The third, Lady Olga Swinton, was a good-looking young woman of twenty-six. She lolled in the corner of the settee with crossed legs, the greater part of which was displayed. When she laughed she threw back her head, showing a firm white throat. A cigarette was in her hand; at intervals she flicked the ash on to the doctor's carpet. The latter, leaning back against the bookcase opposite, surveyed the three with grey eyes that twinkled intelligently. The whole of his lean Scotch face was expressive of humorous kindliness. He was a small, dark, grizzled man of forty-five. His large nose supported a pair of gold-rimmed glasses; his clothes were pleasantly shabby.

In this cabin, sober-hued and somehow less spick, span and glossy than the rest of the ship, were exhibited to their best the colour and freshness of this feminine bunch. Here at least, and for the moment at least, these young women were content with an effect created in common. Sex-consciousness, self-consciousness, the spirit of rivalry, were neutralized by the doctor's personality. And how restful they felt it! They showed it in their faces, in their gestures, and in their merriment which was less than half affected. Whilst flecks of light, thrown up from the rippling water outside, chased each other across the ceiling, whilst the sun-heated air kept the light curtains billowing and flapping, whilst easy jokes and easier laughter bubbled up, unsought —in these moments how pleasant it was to be alive! Yes; and afterwards they would exclaim what a darling Dr. McLaren was. For it was he who made these moments blossom.

Harry, scowling in the doorway, struck quite a discordant note. But the next instant they ignored Harry; they felt strong enough to prolong their mood unchanged; and when they looked again Harry had gone.

A moment later, however, some one else was heard coming along the passage; and at the sound of that step fawn-like Mary stiffened. A young man clad in white drill passed by. Mary continued to take her part in the chatter, but something in her was changed.

After pulling out his watch the doctor drew himself up with determination. Good heavens, nearly a quarter to twelve! He really must be off. But he wasn't going to trust them in his dispensary alone— oh, no! not he! And so . . . But at once three laughing voices answered that not one of them would budge until they had got all the aspirin, phenacetin and veronal they wanted. During the argument, however, Mary slipped away.

Swift, slim, defiantly erect, she marched straight to the wireless office. The young man in white drill stood in the doorway. He replied to the question in her eyes by handing her an envelope. She took it and was gone.

He looked after her, his jaw set. Poor Hugh Stanford! He loved her. It had been his sad fate to succumb even whilst administering to her love for another. No wonder he was inclined to regard the whole universe with a cynicism which, for the moment, did not exclude even Mary herself. For how unkindly swiftly she had plucked the envelope from his hand! Without a word, without a look! Too eager to say even "Thank you!" Too eager even to look shy!

Putting on his topi, he stepped across to the rail and gazed out into the blue-white dazzling milkiness of sky and sea through which the *Clio*, as much aeroplane as ship, was forging. Good God, hadn't he, for her sake, kept this, his etheric domain, fairly buzzing! Hadn't the invisible, the imponderable, the marvellous, and probably non-existent, ether been quivering during the last fortnight, like a jelly, for her sake! Hadn't he, Prospero, kept his Ariels scouting day and night over the whole Atlantic! What rules had he not broken, what conventions not ignored! And his success! Seriously he doubted whether such prodigies of intercommunication had ever been sustained before. Infected with his enthusiasm, every operator in every passing ship had participated; entering into the spirit of the game, every station on the Atlantic seaboard had joined in, to speed forward a message—yet another!—of Mary to Gerald, or Gerald to Mary!

Hugh Stanford grinned sadly. As he leaned over the side the romantic melancholy in his heart linked itself to the wavelets and froth slipping by. For how many years to come would he look down from the deck of a ship on to wavelets and froth indistinguishable from these? And would they not always, always remind him of Mary?

From the captain's quarters there came the sound of laughter. The captain was conversing with the chief engineer and the purser, or, as the latter facetiously styled himself, the hotel manager. For a moment the idea that poor darling Mary's name might be on their lips filled Hugh Stanford with rage. For the fact that Mary was in constant communication with her ineligible young man was an open secret on board. But the next instant he dismissed his suspicions as unjust; he recognised in the men's voices the usual cynical good temper with which these three were accustomed, at this hour, to exchange the news of the day.

At this moment the captain was, in fact, humorously lifting his arms to heaven and asking why, in God's name, her ladyship had suddenly taken the whim to go up the Amazon.

"Well! She's been everywhere else," observed the engineer. And Simpson, the hotel manager, added with a smile:

"That's it. Besides, *she* doesn't really care. She's just agreed to Master Harry's suggestion."

"But why the devil does *he* or anyone else want to go up that beastly river?"

"My dear skipper, no one on board has any particular reason for doing anything. Somebody says, 'Let's go up the Amazon!' and then the others all cry, 'Yes, why not go up the Amazon?'" Simpson laughed genially. "Isn't that about it?"

The captain shrugged. This job under Lady Oswestry was to be his last before retiring. He was drawing fine pay, but he was losing his self-respect. Good God, the courses he had to steer! The chart often looked as if a drunken fly had been crawling over it. In the merchant service—but after all, why deify the merchant service? That was a machine, while her ladyship was a human being—and one that he both liked and respected. A damn fine woman, a woman of character and pluck.

"Well!" said little Simpson, puffing out his chest, "*I* have some work to do. I must be off."

Veeder, the engineer, grinned. "He's got to work out how many more cases of champagne to lay in at Para. Isn't that it, Tommy?"

"No. It's the ship's laundry. The frills on the ladies' undergarments are not being done quite to their liking. I have to look into it."

The two others, who knew their Simpson well, gave him the laugh he expected.

"I'm coming with you," said Veeder.

As they passed out into the sunlight both gave a "Whew!" Here was real tropical heat at last. All the way down from New York they had been lucky in their weather—fine, but with light, cool breezes. This was something different; it took the starch out of you.

Veeder removed his cap and screwed his eyes up at the sun. "Curious thing," said he, "sunstroke is unknown in Brazil. The actinic value of the light is very low. Photographs are generally underexposed."

"That so?" returned Simpson, and they both stopped to watch Lady Oswestry, who at a little distance was taking a snapshot of Sir James Annesley and Hugo.

Chapter 2

AFTER the click the two victims returned to their deck-chairs with a sigh of relief, and Sir James resumed speech at the point at which he had been interrupted. He was talking about Marcel Proust, and his observations were addressed less to Hugo than to a fair young woman who was sitting in a wicker chair opposite. This was Mrs. Barlow, who was regarded by everyone on board as something of a blue stocking. She had been to Girton, and her career there was understood to have been dreadfully distinguished. She had discovered something quite new about atoms; and then, right on the top of this, she had learnt Russian, gone off to Russia, and interviewed Lenin, about whom she had just pub-plished a book.

Sir James always regarded Stella with a certain amusement. For all her brains she had the appearance of being quite a foolish young thing. Indeed, while her age was twenty-five, her expression and complexion remained positively infantile. Her china-blue eyes were limpid with dreaminess; her little white nose looked immature; her lips had the pouting redness of a babe's. She was of medium height and had a graceful figure; but her movements were awkward and so was her manner of speech.

They were sitting under a wide, green awning which

sheltered that part of the deck. A little way off was a table over which a steward was busying himself. It was cocktail time, half an hour or so before lunch, a time marked out for sociability. Lady Oswestry and Olga strolled up, accompanied by Harry and Francis Tilling. The last was a small neat young man with neat small feet and an abundance of neat small talk which he threw out with an air of great *entrain*. Indeed, he had the gift of discharging small hard pellets of speech quite continuously and with such remarkable nonchalance that he seemed to be hardly aware that he was talking.

In the midst of the chatter a servant approached and said something to Harry in a low voice. Harry nodded and presently moved off in the direction of the captain's room.

As he opened the door the conversation within stopped. But when the doctor saw who it was he turned to the captain again and went on. "No, so far as that goes there's nothing to be said. It's the best time of the year—quite the driest season."

The two men were sitting one on each side of the captain's writing desk. Harry lowered himself majestically into an armchair and spread out his big limbs.

"What's the trouble now?" he inquired, cocking an eye at the captain from under his yachting cap.

The latter pursed his lips moodily and said nothing. He was always liverish on first reaching the tropics.

"It's like this, Harry," said the doctor. "The skipper hates giving the *Clio* over to a Dago pilot. And we shall be obliged to have one on board all the time we're in the river."

"Nonsense. It's not that. There's a revolution

going on in Para," growled the captain. "Show his lordship that marconigram, Doctor."

Harry took the paper which the doctor handed him and read it thoughtfully.

"When did this come?"

"Ten minutes ago."

Harry glanced up with a grin. "Damn it all, Captain! You can't grudge them a bit of a revolution now and again—with the rubber trade so dull and all."

The captain looked a trifle sheepish. "We've got ladies on board," he observed.

The doctor eyed him with kindly amusement. "From what I know of South American officials, we shan't be allowed into port, far less up the river, if they're the least bit flustered."

The captain sighed. "Does it really matter to anyone whether we go up that river or not?"

"Matter!" repeated Harry, stretching and yawning. "Why, Captain, the fate of everyone on board depends on it!" He got up and lounged aimlessly about the room. "I'm for another cocktail before lunch. Who'll join me?"

Neither accepted the invitation.

After he had gone the captain began grumbling.

"Well," said he, "you're a clever fellow if you can make Master Harry out. He beats me!"

The doctor's grey eyes glinted humorously. "I don't pretend to make him out, Captain. But I've known him a long time—and I like him, you know."

"Did that last remark of his mean anything? Or was it merely a joke?"

The doctor thought a moment, then said:

"Last night we were talking about chance. He

agreed with me that men's lives are ruled by chance."

The captain shrugged, and went over to the sideboard. "Scotch, neat?—with a chaser?"

"Please. He told me that when he was fifteen—but no! I suppose that was in confidence. Anyhow I reminded him that it was by the merest fluke I ever got to know him or his family."

"How did you get to know them?" asked the captain, suddenly interested.

"It was sixteen—no, seventeen—years ago. I was at Honolulu. And one morning as I was bathing in the surf I saw a party all trying to ride the plank. . . . You know the sport. It's not easy, and of course none of them could do it. Then, as I was swimming round, I saw a big roller come along and snatch one young woman's plank from her and smack her on the head with it. No one else seemed to notice, so it was left to me to drag her out. It was Lady Oswestry. She was stunned; and ill for some days after. I attended her, and there you are."

"She must have been very pretty then," observed the captain slowly.

"By Jove, she was!"

The captain fell into meditation . . .

He was an anxious looking person. From the age of eighteen he had striven to be "a man of iron will." He had gone through life with a set jaw; and the strain of it had left him with little energy for anything else. He had certainly not accomplished much, nor enjoyed himself much. He intended at the end of this cruise to retire into a villa outside Southampton which he had bought with his savings.

He was aware that the villa was not very grand, and that his wife had become extremely stout. Caution had prevented him from having children, and now that it was too late he regretted it. He foresaw that in his retirement he would be rather dull.

Envying the doctor his intimacy with the Oswestrys, he had been curious to learn its origin. He was gratified by what he had heard. That intimacy came of pure chance; the same thing might very well have happened to *him*. The doctor had been luckier; that was all. . . .

But then there flashed into his mind the thought which probably comes into everyone's mind some time or other: Is it worth while to set oneself a goal and go for it with blinkers on and ear-stops in one's ears, when the drifter with the roving eye picks up so many good things on his careless way? Calculation reduces the chances of fair fortune as well as of foul.

And being a man who thought twice before taking a second cup of tea or putting on a clean shirt, the captain did not like the idea that forethought was not the best policy. Could one, he wondered, attain to a degree of cunning which would enable one to reap all the advantages of prudence and yet keep one's net spread open, like any drifter, for the good luck that might be floating by? He pondered; but he kept his thoughts to himself.

The doctor, on his side, had a desire to get up and go away; but, knowing by intuition that his companion was feeling discouraged and envious, he tried to think of something to say to change the captain's mood. It was too hot, however, for mental effort. Moreover, it seemed a pity to fight against the pleasant dreaminess which the whisky had brought on. So at last in silence, but with a friendly nod, he got up and slipped gently out of the room.

As he leant over the side of the ship, his reflections became more and more nebulous under the influence of the light and heat. By turning his head a little to the left he could watch the movements of the brightly clad, cool-looking company under the awning. He wasn't at all sure that civilisation (in the ordinary and slightly gross sense of the word) wasn't the best thing in the world; and that this yacht wasn't the fine flower of civilisation. The democrat, looking on, might grind his teeth with ethical rage; the highbrow might sneer; and the artist fume; but the fact remained that the air of Mayfair was sweeter than that of Hampstead, Bloomsbury, or Chelsea. It was convenient to draw on Hampstead for convictions, on Bloomsbury for ideas, and on Chelsea for drawing-room topics; but more than that. . . . And he stretched himself till his joints cracked.

The company under the awning had begun to drift in to lunch. A big punkah moved slowly backwards and forwards across the saloon. The table was decorated with flowers from Jamaica, which had been hibernating in cold storage. A cool dew still clung to them. They were scentless, but a perfume went up from the human beings gathered round. The doctor caught a whiff of it as, presently, he passed the open door. Some day, he reflected, men would learn to give its due to the sense of smell. The smell which the punkah wafted forth was human —human, but not too human; warm and yet fresh—

a smell delicate and composite; artificial because soaps, perfumes, powders, tobacco, hair lotions and sachet-scented fabrics entered into it; but naturalised and blended into unity by the odour of the human body; a smell of men and women living in the highest possible state of cleanliness; the smell of the fine flower of civilisation.

Immersed in this atmosphere it was well-nigh impossible not to respond with a sense of social exhilaration. Neither the pretty faces nor the pretty dresses, nor the talking, nor the laughing probably contributed so much. "Without doubt," mused the doctor, "our olfactory nerves play a much larger part in our lives than we imagine. It is not to be believed that the sense of smell, which is of paramount importance to most animals, is insignificant in man. I should not be surprised if our subconsciousness were largely governed by it. The reason why I do not love Dr. Fell is that his smell is displeasing to me."

As the meal went on and the temperature of the room rose, the animation of the company increased. Not very much attention, however, was given to the food nor to the wine, excellent though they both were. The minds of Lady Oswestry's guests were otherwise occupied. In the first place they were aware of themselves as a social group with certain standards to keep up; and, secondly, each felt he had to hold his own in the group. It is true the sense of effort was, in most cases, not great, for the effort had become more or less instinctive and was made more or less unwittingly. But the effort was none the less there.

Chapter 3

MEANWHILE the good ship *Clio* was forging steadily ahead. The warm, smooth sea lay all around her for leagues and leagues. The mainland of South America was still more than fifty miles away. But the sun, right overhead, looked down upon a water that was no longer salt and clear. Even at this distance it was heavily tainted by the prodigious disgorgement of the Amazon.

No breeze, no porpoise, no flying-fish, ruffled the greenish-yellow liquid across which the *Clio* was cutting her bright way. No other vessel was in sight. No bird, no insect, was in the sky. The *Clio* alone existed here. And she moved swiftly, evenly, unvaryingly, like a sun travelling through its own private section of the universe.

There was purpose and power in her onward movement just as there was grace in her lines, and smoothness, cleanliness, and polish over her entire surface. She not only gleamed and glittered, but she was strong and efficient. She resembled a great mechanical fish; she was like a magical toy constructed for a princess's pleasure. It was fitting that strains of music should rise above the low deep hum of her turbines, that she should trail behind her frills and flounces of foam, and that the breeze of her passage should be suffused with a faint, not unpleasing scent.

The music which accompanied her at this hour emanated, however (let us make the admission without false shame) from no more elegant an instrument than a concertina. A very common little tune was being played in the stern by one of the crew. He was a fine specimen; indeed all the sailors on board the *Clio* were—like the rest of her fittings—the best on the market. Looking down on the concertina player and his fellows lying smoking on a shaded portion of the lower deck, one could not but liken them to prize pigs in a sty. And the comparison was all to their advantage, for they looked happier and more intelligent than pigs. They were fat, it is true, but not unhealthy. If they ate well it was because they were able to digest well. What class is better able to assimilate nourishing food than sailors? Sea air stimulates metabolism, the appetite responds, a vigorous liver co-operates, the healthy mind reflects the vacancy of the circumambient horizon; there is everything to promote, and nothing to impede, the enormous digestive capacities which the sea developes in her children. All mammals that take to a sea life acquire girth and placidity; witness the whale, the sea-elephant, and the dugong or sea-cow. As for the *Clio's* crew—well! look at those buttocks! look at that forearm, and especially at the back of that neck! Mark closely that neck! The necks of able-bodied seamen on expensive yachts well repay a careful study. Measure the breadth and compare it first with the breadth of the back of the head and, secondly, with the breadth of the forehead. Prod it next with your finger and note the peculiar resiliency. Observe the deep rich colour, and examine the grain of the skin. Necks such as this tell their simple story with conciseness and eloquence.

On this portion of the deck and within these lumps of brick-red flesh amazing feats of digestion and assimilation were being accomplished. These worthy fellows, lying about like seals on a floe, looked inactive, but in truth they were not. And if one of them belched occasionally, it was done out of pure sociability.

Behind them in the galley there was the clatter of washing up. Stewards, creatures of a paler, lighter breed, were wiping plates and conversing amiably in grumbling Cockney tones. They grumbled and cursed, they railed and mocked at their masters; they complained of overwork and underpay—all quite good-humouredly. For all were aware that their present billet was an uncommonly good one.

A little further along the passage was the lady's maids' room, out of which came a smell of ironed linen, orris-root, and lavender. In this room two or three young women were generally to be found gossiping together or, if not gossiping, enjoying the pleasures of perfect unrestraint. The maid who in the presence of her mistress was most genteel, most mincing, most breathlessly respectful, here generously made up for it. Here she would fling herself about, bang things about, and shout out her words with the vulgarest accent at her command.

It pleased nearly every one of them to act thus at times; and although, in general, not very fond of each other, they enjoyed each other's society—principally perhaps for the sake of these manifestations. Not for the world would these girls have displayed such manners before superiors, nor before inferiors, nor even before their parents at home. At home each girl took a pleasure in being amazingly ladylike. And yet the secret revolt against this ladylikeness persisted. Wherever there is discipline, even though it be self-discipline, an underground resentfulness persists. There may be a pleasure in the observance of the discipline and a pride in the results obtained, but still it persists.

If the servants on the *Clio* were well-satisfied, it was not only on account of the pay, but also because they enjoyed to the full the prestige reflected upon them by their employers. Most of the guests on board were quite accustomed to being photographed for the weekly illustrated papers. The *Clio* herself and the whole assembled party had been thus honoured at New York and again at Kingston. Moreover, at whatever port they touched a flattering paragraph appeared in the local Press. These things counted not a little; they fostered a spirit of solidarity and self-respect.

So now in the damp lazy heat of the afternoon a contented slumberousness spread over the ship. The sea offers a glorious relief from responsibility. Home may be burning, wife starving, children dying of croup, but what, on the high seas, can father, be he never so devoted, do? Nothing! Happily nothing!

It is not only, however, by severing a man from his past that the ocean bestows rest upon him. It refreshes him equally by dulling his thought for the future. On land the present is apt to be merely the moving point at which the anxious future is swallowed up by the uninteresting past. On the high seas the present has extension. It waxes large and fat and heavy. Life on land is then seen to be little more than a sequence of preparations and expectancies. On shipboard a man expects nothing and is without forethought or curiosity. How many of the human beings on the *Clio* gave a moment's consideration to the continent which they were approaching? Of the women not one; and of the men not more than two or three. It was true, the conversation at luncheon had turned for a few minutes upon the Amazon. But that not inconsiderable river had been incapable of holding the attention of anyone; it had served as a passing topic—nothing more. And why should it have been otherwise? What in the world is sillier than the intelligent interest trumped up by the unintelligent tourist to carry him along his aimless way? What is he—what can he be—but a perambulating stare. Moreover, there is little to choose—in the matter of parochialism—between the farm labourer and the travelled man of the world. The former ignores the things outside his village, the latter what lies outside a few thousands miles of space, a few hundred years of time. Lady Oswestry, who was too intelligent a woman to cultivate philosophic pretensions, wasted no time on South America beyond wondering whether it would be possible to obtain at Para a particular kind of face cream of which she was running short. The cook wondered what green vegetables he would be able to buy there; and—with two or three exceptions—the thoughts of the others, if they fluttered landwards, went there upon errands of a similar nature.

The question of the face cream was, however, really of the highest importance. Lady Oswestry had run short once before and her skin had immediately suffered. No other preparation suited her, and in the tropics one had to be specially careful. It was Jane's fault that her stock had not been replenished at New York; at Havana the shop assistant had made a mistake; and in the other places the cream had been unobtainable. Her hopes now centred on Para. It would be too bad if an idiotic little revolution were to prevent a landing there. At lunch she suggested to Harry that they should make for Rio de Janeiro if Para were impossible; and Harry staggered her by replying that Rio was about three thousand miles further on.

"The United States of Brazil," Sir James informed everybody, "comprise twenty provinces, of which at least eleven are larger than Britain. Brazil, in fact, is quite a big place."

Lady Oswestry looked meditative.

"Why not go up the Orinoco, if the Amazon is barred?" suggested Francis brightly. "Simpson says the crocodiles there are even bigger."

"So tiresome of Para to revolt just when we're coming!" said Olga.

"Well, well!" Sir James's voice was indulgent. "The Federal Government is rather weak, you see, and extremely greedy in its taxation, and a considerable way off. And there's really nothing else to do on the Amazon now that the rubber industry is dead."

Lady Oswestry did not pursue the subject. She knew that Harry would do anything he could to please her. If it were humanly possible to obtain that face cream at Para, Harry would do it. But she hadn't spoken to him on the matter yet. She was always slightly shy with Harry—simply because the link between them was so strong. And yet Harry rather frightened her. She couldn't understand him. She couldn't manage him as she could the sweet, limpid, reasonable Hugo. All his life Harry had caused her pain. She was ambitious for him, and he seemed to enjoy disappointing her. His foible was playing the buffoon.

Well! Harry was now thirty, and she had been obliged to give him up. She had focused her ambitions upon Hugo, who had no objection to making himself a career. Sir James was going to help; he already looked upon Hugo as a son. It made her heart expand with pleasure to watch them pacing the deck together: Hugo in all the glory of his fresh ruddy youth, and the other looking so unobtrusively, and yet so completely, what every man of his age (nearly sixty) would choose to look, were it possible.

"What if we had met earlier and married . . . ?" Sometimes she pondered this. But without vain regrets. It was unlikely that he would have proposed to her thirty years ago, and unlikely that she would then have accepted him, if he had. They were both too ambitious. He wouldn't have burdened himself with a wife. Certainly not with the third daughter of an impoverished squire. And she, well! she had felt that money was the first essential. So she had married Lord Oswestry, who was just twice her age. It was not her fault if, seven years later, her husband lost most of his fortune—and in a rather shady affair, too.

The disaster had put her on her mettle. Lord Oswestry, now past middle-age, had felt inclined to step out of the arena. But she wouldn't have it. She fought a long fight for the restoration of his financial, and her social, position. And in the end she won. But how she had had to intrigue, and bluff, and lie! Yes, and to suffer smilingly many a slight and rebuff. But now it was all over; and neither good spirits, generosity, not intrinsic honesty had been lost. She harboured no bitterness. She could look round her table at these girls who were half her age and find nothing but kindliness in her heart. She didn't ask herself whether they had her courage, her energy, or her perseverance. For she was modest. She attributed her success almost entirely to her face and figure. A woman had to work through men, and what counted with men was the trim ankle and the clear skin. There was no cynicism in a constatation so obvious. God had blessed her in her legs and in her complexion, and she was grateful. That muddle in regard to the face cream made her ashamed. It would serve her right if she failed in her present design. She wanted to marry Sir James. She needed him for Hugo. Thus only could she make sure of securing his best services for as long as he lived. Sir James was an angel, and devoted to her—always had been; but she had to make sure that he would *go on* being an angel—to her and to Hugo, and not to anyone else.

This little cruise was a critical manœuvre in her plan of campaign. Was the want of that face cream going to injure Hugo's future career? She was a woman of too much imagination and experience to scout this anxiety as fantastic. Would Sir James marry her if her cheeks became rough and pimply? Alas! the imperfections to which love is blind are not as a rule the physical ones. Nor did she make the mistake of imagining that Sir James prized beauty less for having reached the age to know that it was skin deep.

As she watched him talking to Mary she could tell just how well the shape of Mary's little ear pleased him. She knew just how he adored the lovely olive tint of Mary's neck, and the soft line where the first downy hairs came out of that polished smoothness. Nor was she vexed. She approved his taste. Besides, the exterior was so often a true reflection of what lay within. In Mary this was signally the case. Fine, taut, eager, Mary both looked and was. Pride was now making her laugh and chatter, but there were instants when the pain in her eyes showed that she had forgotten everyone, forgotten where she was. And Lady Oswestry knew that Sir James was longing with all a man's sentimentality that Mary might have her Gerald. "What does it matter if he is a scamp? Can't you see, my dear, that anyone who wants anything as much as that ought to have it?"

After lunch, as they were taking their coffee under the awning, she noticed Mary get up and slip away. "Poor darling!" she thought. "Our company has become intolerable. I wish I could go and comfort her, but I know I mustn't. If she had wanted to talk, she would have come to me herself before now."

At that moment Stella Barlow leaned forward and said in an undertone:

"Mary has been looking a bit strained. Did you notice? I'm afraid she must have had bad news."

"Was there another marconigram for her this morning?"

"Yes—so Angela says."

Lady Oswestry was silent. She was sorry that Mary had no confidant on board.

"Shall I go down to her?" asked Stella.

"I wish you would."

"I shall probably get snubbed."

"Never mind," replied Lady Oswestry with a smile. Stella was the member of her party whom she knew least well. But she liked Stella; there was something honest about her.

Stella's knock at Mary's door was answered quickly and sharply.

She found Mary sitting on the edge of the bed.

"May I really come in? I had a sudden wish to talk to you. Do you mind?" She was not exactly shy in spite of Mary's stare, but she did feel somewhat gauche.

"Awfully sweet of you!" returned Mary in a completely expressionless voice.

"Olga and Francis are unendurable when they once get started," Stella went on. She walked over to the porthole, and while pretending to look out, studied Mary out of the tail of her eye. Mary sat still, with a white face, gazing straight at the wall.

She was too miserable to take notice. Stella waited.

"I suppose," Mary murmured, "they are all busy discussing me up there."

"No," replied Stella, "they wouldn't — not publicly."

Mary gave a little snort of indifference.

"Why did you come on this cruise?" asked Stella with bluntness. "Lady Oswestry didn't kidnap you."

Mary was silent for a moment, then she said:

"I had a quarrel with Gerald. I accepted in order to annoy him. But I only intended to go as far as New York. . . . I was going to return on the *Berengaria*."

"Have you settled your quarrel yet?"

"Oh, yes. We made it up by wireless just after I started on this cruise south. I was an idiot to come." Whilst speaking she never moved nor detached her eyes from the wall. Stella studied her with the greatest curiosity. It was interesting to be in the presence of some one whose heart and soul were completely absent. She pitied Mary and yet she didn't pity her. It was difficult to feel sympathy for the girl who was not disguising the fact that she was indifferent to the whole of her present surroundings. Stella saw that deep down in her heart Mary was living a solitary far-away life of her own. Moreover, she was living on quite a different level of intensity from anyone else on board. "C'est magnifique," said Stella to herself, "mais ce n'est pas la vie." People who are in love are as remote as lunatics.

"Well, if you two have made it up . . ." she hazarded.

Mary's lips moved in a little bitter smile.

There was a photograph of Gerald on the table. It showed a slim, handsome young man in the uniform of a flying officer. Gerald had distinguished himself in the war, but not since.

"I had another message from him this morning. He is making a fool of himself again." And Mary dug her fingers into the bed.

"How?"

"He's started for Havana via New York. He wants to meet me there on our return voyage. That means he's thrown away his job and borrowed money for the journey."

Stella found nothing to say. Mary leant back on one elbow and for the first time turned her head. The thin, dark line of her eyebrows expressed a melancholy amusement.

"Gerald can't wait. I'm not very good at waiting myself. But Gerald! . . . This'll give everybody the opportunity of saying, 'There! Look what he's done now!' But it's my fault really. I only came on this cruise because he'd annoyed me so." And she gave her low brief laugh which was at once so disillusioned and so innocent.

"He talks about joining the *Clio* by hydroplane from Havana," Mary went on disdainfully. "Can you imagine it? He probably hasn't even glanced at a map. He'll kill himself."

She was looking down and plucking at the coverlet. He doesn't fly as well as he used," she added. "He landed me in a tree the other day."

Suddenly she sprang to her feet and began walking up and down. "My God!" she exclaimed, "if only one's parents could understand that their children are utterly unlike them. . . . I shall never be able to forgive mother and father for this. If *my* daughter wanted to marry a Hottentot I'd help her. What does it matter if Gerald hasn't any money? I've got lots. Or if he were to run after other women later on? He wouldn't, because I wouldn't let him. And what would it matter if he did? Life can't be lived in the way one's parents think. . . . That's all done with. People are different now."

Not once while she was speaking had she looked at Stella, who was at last beginning to feel slightly awkward. She and Mary, she found, had no natural sympathy for one another. In a way they made a contact; but no spark came from the contact, no sympathy flashed up on either side.

Mary, however, now turned to Stella with a sudden smile of contrition. "I'm so sorry," she murmured. "I've been terribly boring. It was *too* nice of you to come."

Stella's reply was interrupted by a knock at the door, and one of the stewardesses, a stout middle-aged woman, bustled into the room. On seeing Stella there she stopped short in surprise; but after an instant's hesitation she did not withdraw but began putting away in the chest of drawers an armful of clean linen which she had brought in.

"My! the heat we're running into now. I shall have a stroke, I know I will. That's what comes of being fat. Though it's not for want of running about. You ought to be in bed, Miss Mary. In bed and asleep till five o'clock. That's the rule in the tropics." As she ran on, Stella could see that between her and Mary there existed that natural animal link for want of which her own intercourse with Mary was doomed to sterility. Here were two persons as unlike to one another as you could conceive. There was every inequality of birth, breeding, age and intellect to sunder them; yet their sympathy was complete. Upon a basis of inequality it flourished secure.

Chapter 4

AFTER leaving Mary Stella went slowly down the passage to her own cabin, locked the door behind her and examined herself in the glass. She wished that she had been given a face and figure more like Mary's. It was true that in some ways she was prettier, but Mary had style. Mary looked much more finished. Most people, she reflected sadly, did so lack finish. They looked terribly shop-soiled and untidy and misshapen. One had to fall back upon their moral qualities in order not to dislike them.

With a sigh she slowly unfastened her dress and let it drop to her feet. Slowly she divested herself of all but her chemise and stockings. Then she looked at the clock, hastily powdered her face, unlocked the door and got into bed.

Punctually at three-thirty the door opened and closed again behind Hugo. Whilst turning the key in the lock he looked over his shoulder at Stella with a shy smile. The young woman was sitting up with her hands clasped behind her head, her babyish face had a bored, slightly contemptuous expression.

"Why are we going at half-speed?" she asked, speaking in a low voice.

He replied in the same tone. "At half-speed?

Are we?" He had begun walking towards the bed,
but now he turned his steps to the porthole. "So
we are."

"And if I were to ask someone who knew I should
only be told some lie."

"I suppose so."

"The government of a ship and the government
of a nation——" began Stella, and then stopped
with a gesture of utter boredom.

Hugo came and sat down on the edge of the bed.
He wore white silk pyjamas with light blue cuffs
and collar. His smile was now a trifle self-conscious.
Slipping one arm round her waist, he bent forward
and gave her a kiss which fell upon her neck, for
she had rapidly averted her face. At the touch of
his lips, however, her looks grew tender and at the
same time sad. But only for a moment; almost at
once she pushed him away.

"Thank you. I'm quite hot enough as it is.
Hadn't you better go and sit over there? I want
to talk."

Hugo, slightly discountenanced, did as he was bid.

"I must tell you something," said Stella. "I
haven't the slightest doubt left that your mother
knows all about—this."

Hugo frowned and made a puzzled gesture.

"She certainly didn't know——"

"When she invited me, no. But I think she
must have found out pretty soon afterwards."

Hugo looked up at the ceiling and sighed. It was
very quiet in the cabin. The engines turning at
half-speed made a hum that was scarcely audible.
Presently, looking straight before her, Stella said:

"Your mother is afraid that you may marry me."

"Your husband is still alive," replied Hugo after a slight pause.

"Yes, but if he goes on as he is doing now he's not likely to live much longer."

"And you think my mother knows that?"

Stella shook her shoulders like a sulky child. "Good Lord, yes. She knows everything she wants to know. What I can't understand is why she ever asked me on board. No!" she went on with one of her sudden changes of tone, "I don't mean that. She invited me because she rather likes me. And I feel a bit small for having accepted—in the circumstances. It's quite plain to me now that she wants you to marry Olga."

Hugo was looking rather uncomfortable.

"She knows I won't marry Olga—not even to please her."

"No, no, but you very well might for the sake of your precious career. And that's one of the reasons why I couldn't marry you myself. I'm sick of your career already. To be your wife is too awful to imagine. But Olga would lend herself to it admirably. She'd make up to the right people for you, and give political dinners, and open bazaars, to perfection. She looks the part, and she dresses to the part, and she'd enjoy the part. If ever you flagged she'd boost you on, and all her smart relatives would be cajoled into boosting you on."

"Olga's relatives aren't smart," replied Hugo, making what rejoinder he could, for he was distinctly nettled. "That's just what worries her. They ought to be smart considering what birth and brains they have; but they aren't smart at all. They are positively dowdy."

"They are just the people to boost you on. Don't wander from the point, Hugo."

"What is the point precisely?"

"Your career. Everything centres on that. Harry has been given up as a bad job. Your mother sees she can't manage Harry. But she can manage you. This cruise was arranged simply for the sake of your career. Sir James——"

"For heaven's sake don't shout."

"There's never been a better wire-puller than Sir James, has there? Well, that's why he's here. Your mother and he are planning their campaign, step by step—what private secretaryships you shall have, what constituencies you shall stand for, what your battle-cries shall be, etc., etc. And every single wire that Sir James holds is going to be pulled for you."

"Go on! I don't mind."

"It began when you were already a boy at Eton, as you let out to me the other day. Although you didn't really care about anything but sculling, and weren't particularly bright at your books, you were made to write semi-political articles for the *Eton Chronicle*, and to wriggle your way up to be President of the School Debating Society. And exactly the same thing happened at Oxford. So that you finally managed to get yourself elected Vice-President of the Union."

"All right," said Hugo imperturbably. "But what's all this leading up to. Why shouldn't I have a political career?"

Stella, who was now quite pink, glared at him

with her china-blue eyes like an infuriated doll.
" No, why not? Politics is about all you're
good for."

" I don't know why you should always end up by
being so infernally rude to me," observed Hugo,
looking up at the ceiling.

" Oh, it's because I'm so middle-class, I suppose.
People like you, born with titles and silver spoons
in their mouths, annoy me. . . . People who sit
still all their lives, smiling complacently, while others
are boosting them up the political tree! "

" I know. You prefer the Lenin type. You're
really very feminine, my dear. You're a worshipper
of the strong man."

" I certainly have the poor taste to prefer strong
men to weak ones. And as for Lenin——"

"You consider his illness and death a real tragedy
for the human race. I know. I've been reading
your book at last. It's not so badly written
considering . . . "

He became very boyish when he tried to hit back,
and Stella now smiled indulgently. But there was,
as she knew, another side of his character which was
by no means boyish. Hugo had a fund of worldly
shrewdness which she could only regard as part of
his inheritance. It was innate. That worldly wisdom
did not, however, detract from his uprightness. He
was very like his mother in this respect. With all
her gaiety and carelessness Lady Oswestry had never
missed a chance in life. Stella had heard all about
her from Francis and Angela, who had her history
at their fingers' ends. Hugo's career would resemble
his mother's; he would reach success.

But to fight the world with its own weapons under the old familiar rules, and for the usual prizes, was a game that did not appeal to Stella. She was at heart a revolutionary. She was fond of Hugo, but he irritated her. He was too well-balanced.

Keeping her eyes off him (for she thought him exceedingly attractive in his white silk pyjamas), she said dryly :

"Do you know where Jock is at this moment?"

Jock was her husband.

"No," replied Hugo.

"Exactly. You've never been sufficiently interested to ask me where he was."

"I knew he was abroad," said Hugo gently.

"What else did you know?"

"Well! That he drank."

"Anything else?"

Hugo thought for a moment. "No."

"Would you like to know whether I still care about him?"

"I've always imagined you didn't—much," replied Hugo cautiously.

Stella laughed.

"Well! to come back to the question of where he is. He's at Para."

"Oh, dear!" said Hugo, startled.

Stella, who was now looking at him hard, laughed again.

"I like to set your great brain in motion once in a while," said she. "I like giving it a shake—as one shakes a clock that has stopped because it needs cleaning. It goes tick, tick, tick for five minutes or so and then settles down into lethargy again."

"You think my mother knew this?" asked Hugo slowly.

"Yes, I do. At least, it's a possibility, isn't it?"

"But how should she know about your husband's movements?"

"Jock has always been at Para. I mean he hasn't left the place since he left me. His only 'movements' are from one bar to another."

"Yes. She may be aware of it," said Hugo uncomfortably. "Harry may have told her."

"Harry? Does Harry know everything?" inquired Stella with sarcasm.

Hugo made no reply.

"If you want to know," continued Stella, "I've always looked upon Harry as rather a joke."

"Oh, yes," sighed Hugo. "He *is* a bit of a joke. But that's largely his pose. At bottom, he is much more than a joke—is Harry."

"I'm so glad you have a black sheep in your family. I wish Harry would do something really outrageous."

"You wish he *would*. . . . My God! as if——" He checked himself.

"Oh, go on," begged Stella.

Hugo shook his head. For a couple of minutes he meditated, while Stella continued to watch him.

"It's quite possible that we shan't put into Para at all," he murmured at last.

"Do you really think so? Owing to this revolution?" Her voice betrayed disappointment. "I've just been reading about the Amazon. And I was getting rather keen on it. I feel that something might happen to us up there."

Hugo smiled. " Nothing will happen to us. We're much too well managed."

" Oh, my God ! " murmured Stella disgustedly. And she added : " That's just what I object to about you all. You're much too careful—for all your apparent carelessness." She kicked about under the sheet like a pettish child. " Why on earth *not* go up the Amazon—in spite of the revolution ? "

" It is quite possible that we shall just turn and go back," repeated Hugo with a touch of malice.

" I wonder how that would affect Mary," said Stella, suddenly pensive.

" Poor dear Mary ! " smiled Hugo.

Stella's blue eyes flashed at him in real indignation. " Oh, yes ! You *would* laugh ! You don't know— and don't want to know—what love is."

" All right then. I don't."

" That's honest at any rate." She melted suddenly and held out her hand. " Come here, Hugo."

He came and sat on the edge of the bed. She gazed deep into his eyes. She murmured appealingly. " What shall I say to Jock ? " And with a sigh she added : " What is your mother up to, Hugo ? "

He didn't answer. He couldn't mix business with pleasure. At this moment she was making a physical appeal to him, and he resented being called upon to think. He bent and gave her a long kiss, which she made no pretence of evading. But after a few moments of warm amorous silence she repeated her questions, and although her voice was dreamy, he knew she required an answer.

Drawing himself up, he looked over her head thoughtfully. Her persistence caused him a keen inward annoyance, but he was taking great pains not to let it show.

"I really don't think my mother is 'up to' anything in particular," he replied at last. "If you're looking for a motive for this trip to the Amazon. . . . But really you needn't!"

"Yes, but if I do?"

He made a gesture. "Well, you might take Harry's banana plantations as a motive. He's got immense plantations about ten miles up from Para."

"Oh," she said, still dreamy. "I never knew that." And she ran her hand up his arm under the wide sleeve of his pyjamas.

He paid no attention to the caress. He wasn't in that mood any longer, and it was her fault.

"I must be off. It's nearly five. We've spent all our time talking."

She detected the "There now! And serve you right!" in his voice. So after lifting her head to glance at her clock she gave a pretended start of surprise. "Heavens! And I promised to make a fourth at bridge."

"At five? You'll have to hurry." And with another perfunctory kiss he left her.

She dressed quickly and went up to see whether she could turn her invented bridge engagement into reality. She succeeded; when Hugo appeared the rubber had just begun.

Hugo strolled over to where his mother and Sir James were sitting, and picked up from her lap the little typewritten sheet on which Hugh Stanford served up daily such news as he was able to collect.

"Anything interesting?" he murmured.

Sir James looked up at him lazily. "Nothing. The news becomes less interesting every day as we become more detached. Besides, nothing is interesting without details—I might almost say *except* details—which one naturally doesn't get."

"All the same, what's this!" exclaimed Hugo. "Turpentine! Did you see this about turpentine?"

"No."

"You know there's a corner in turps?" And Hugo looked at Sir James meaningly.

"Yes, yes."

"Well! there's something about it here."

Lady Oswestry had a faint, slightly mischievous smile on her face. "Perhaps that's the reason why Harry rushed off to the wireless office after lunch."

Hugo glanced down, nodded, and gave a laugh. "A mysterious fellow, Harry! Full of secrets." And he strolled away.

"I wonder if Harry's making *another* fortune," said Sir James.

"I shouldn't be at all surprised." And Lady Oswestry rather strangely sighed. "He's frightfully clever at business, you know."

They conversed in the manner of those who have infinite leisure before them. Lady Oswestry held up the jumper that she was knitting and looked at it with a frown. "What's thirty-two and sixteen?"

"Forty-eight."

"Thank you. And thirty-four and fourteen are also forty-eight. That's right."

"It's a pity that Harry has always refused to employ his gifts in other directions."

"Yes. But I've stopped worrying about that, my dear James. After all he must live as he chooses —so long as he doesn't do anything too awful." And she glanced up from her knitting with the little careless laugh that had pleased him so much twenty years ago.

His thoughts travelled back. What a pity it was that he had not met her before her marriage. But supposing he had married her himself, could he have kept her? She was uncommonly wild in those days. It would have been a ticklish business. She might have helped him in his career, as she had helped old Oswestry. But he could never have endured what old Oswestry had had to put up with. Not that Oswestry hadn't played a wise part. Cunning old devil! Nobody had ever been able to say whether he knew—whether he even suspected—how much he owed to his wife. What with his short sight, and his deafness—probably both more than half put on—and his general air of imbecility, you never could tell what he was, and what he wasn't, taking in. There was certainly precious little he missed when looking at a horse, or a prospectus, or even an hotel bill.

"If Mary doesn't reappear soon, I think you ought to go down and look her up," he said with a yawn.

She regarded him curiously. "That's the first time I've ever seen you yawn, James."

"It's the tropics. In temperate climes I never yawn except on purpose."

"As a snub."

"Yes. Aren't you worried about Mary?"

"Terribly!" replied Lady Oswestry with a serene

sigh. "Poor darling! She nearly breaks my heart."

"Is Gerald so very undesirable?"

"A good deal more undesirable than most young men."

"My dear Marion, I thought any and every young man was desirable nowadays."

"Hardly for a creature like Mary, do you think? She's so very exceptional."

"She'll marry him. No one can stop her."

"I quite agree," replied Lady Oswestry, laughing gently. "And I wouldn't have taken her away—I wouldn't have delayed their marriage by a day—if I'd known that she was going to be so miserable. But her mother begged me to remove her, and Mary herself seemed ready to come."

Sir James was silent.

"It's curious that she should be fretting to this extent," Lady Oswestry went on. "She knows she'll see her young man again when she gets back. She's only got to wait."

"There are some people who cannot wait," said Sir James with unusual emphasis.

Lady Oswestry glanced up.

"Some people can wait and some people can't," continued Sir James. "People with imagination often can't."

"Because?"

"Because they realise only too well what changes and chances there are in our mortal life."

Lady Oswestry's eyes rested on him affectionately. "Dear James! I can see you've really taken Mary's cause to heart. Whenever you talk about her you become quite moved, don't you?"

"And because they feel—deep down—that they themselves may change," Sir James went on.

"But wouldn't it be a good thing if Mary's affections did change?"

Sir James kept his gaze fixed upon the horizon. "It would be a death—the death of something—silly perhaps, but beautiful in its way."

"Shall I turn the *Clio's* nose straight home now?"

"No. *Che sara sara*. And in this you have to be on the side of common sense."

"Harry!" called Lady Oswestry. And Harry, who was passing by, swerved over in her direction. "How is it going—the gamble?"

Harry gave a long stare. "God knows!" he grumbled out at last.

"Is it important?"

"Oh, no!"

It might be the truth. You never could tell, because Harry dealt out truth and lies quite indiscriminately. Mother and son looked each other humorously in the eyes.

"Hugh Stanford oughter—get the sack," jerked out Harry.

"Oh, no! Why?"

"Spends his time playing the fool—instead of attending to business."

Hugo had come up and was listening with a smile. He put his hand on his mother's shoulder. "I think I know what he means."

And as Harry lounged off, he went on: "Stanford gives Mary preference over everything else. You know the wireless works best at night. Well, he's often up till dawn trying to get Mary's messages through. Then, next day, he's sleepy and—there you are!"

Sir James and Lady Oswestry looked at one another smilingly, while Hugo strolled across the deck to watch the bridge players.

Chapter 5

THE *Clio* was now gliding slowly through a greenish-yellow water which was broken by short choppy waves and an occasional splash of foam. This surface commotion was caused less by the evening breeze than by the clash of river current and tide swell over a shallow bottom. The ship's bows pointed south. Before her was a semi-transparent sheet of golden mist which stretched up from the sea to the zenith. Dusk was gathering; the sudden spectacular close of the day was at hand.

It was the hour at which couples would rise and begin pacing the deck. Lady Oswestry and Sir James got up; she slipped her hand under his arm; without speech they fell into step.

A flare of splendid colours had broken out in the west; deep purple clouds stood hooded in melancholy against a passionate background of orange and red. It suggested a drama of despair—a drama enacted by the elemental deities of the earth.

The drama flamed in silence. It painted the sky with tokens of protest, rage and grief. Its colours fell upon the lonely water, touching it with lights that soon would fade; for darkness was creeping on—like death, like cold faintness and oblivion stealing over a spirit still hot, still avid, for all the ardours and all the pains of life.

Sir James had been in India as a young man. O God! these tropical sunsets! What was the secret of their influence over him now? Did they stir some buried memory? If not, why was it that every evening at sundown he was seized with a distress so poignant that he positively feared for his sanity. Some sorrow within him reared its head. . . . Like a sea-monster. . . . What was it? And whence? And why? He looked into himself aghast. He stared in consternation at his inexplicable torment.

Lady Oswestry was dreamy. He walked at her side, a being dumb with anguish. At last, murmuring some excuse, he left her. He went and took a whisky and soda in the saloon with the genial Tommy Simpson. The hotel manager—God bless him!—was always full of cheerful conversation. Gradually the nightmare lifted. In a little while he was able to rejoin Lady Oswestry on deck, but he took Simpson with him.

Leaning over the rail, he commented upon the fact that the *Clio* was now going dead slow.

"Yes, that's because we're almost there," returned Simpson. "We're looking out for the Atalaya light. As soon as we've got it we shall anchor for the night."

"What about the revolution?"

"Ho ho!" laughed Simpson. "There's no revolution. Hasn't his lordship told you? That was a mare's nest."

Harry, who was pacing the deck by himself, came up to where they were standing.

"I got a message from Schmidt—not ten minutes ago—'Welcome to Para,' If there's a revolution on, he hasn't noticed it."

Lady Oswestry sighed with relief. "They say that Para is a little Paris," she murmured.

"It wanted to be," replied Harry, as he strolled off again.

Together the others walked forward and peered into the greyness. The sun's rusty glow had faded out of the air; it was mistily dark.

"To-morrow morning at dawn we shall signal the pilot," continued Simpson. "As soon as we get him aboard we start down the estuary. That light ought to be showing up soon; although——" He interrupted himself to listen to a shout from a sailor who was up aloft. "That's it! We've fetched up Atalaya. Pretty good work considering the mist—*and* the current *and* the tide. We've been approaching from due north, cutting right across the river's chief outlets; it's one of the trickiest bits of coast I know. And his lordship insisted on keeping in close because he was in a hurry to get to Para."

"Then why don't we go down the estuary to-night? The liners do it."

"Why don't we? I don't know, Sir James! Except that Lord Oswestry is apparently no longer in a hurry. And Captain Wilson would just as soon lie here till daybreak. As a matter of fact we've already touched bottom twice to-day."

"Oh, have we!" said Sir James, drily.

"Only mud—lovely soft mud," laughed Simpson reassuringly. "Do you know, Sir James, how much mud the Amazon brings down every twenty-four hours? Twenty to thirty-five million tons, sir! Yes, sir, every day! But for the tide sweep there'd be a delta sticking out half-way across the South

Atlantic. But the current northwards is tremendous. The mud gets shifted here and there; shoal one day, deep water the next. And it's like that all the way down to Para—another eighty miles or so."

Sir James put up his night glasses and gazed at the light; he felt peaceful again. His dangerous hour had gone by. Simpson saluted and strutted off.

"Nice little fellow, that," he murmured.

His elbow touched his companion's as they leaned together over the rail. Behind them the lights of the saloon were shining brightly. A group had gathered round the piano; Francis Tilling was beginning to sing. His big deep voice contrasted comically with his lean little dandy's body. He liked best passionate airs from the Italian Opera; but, having found that these always brought on fits of giggling, he now refused to sing anything " serious."

As the singing, talking and laughing waxed louder and louder a smile gathered on Lady Oswestry's face. It began at the lips and mounted slowly to the eyes until her whole face was illuminated. And yet the smile remained faint, exquisitely faint, almost tender —as if it were the bloom upon a delicate inward sadness. Sir James loved that smile of hers. And at this moment it affected him quite particularly. For by what had it been evoked? By the gaiety of young girls.

He drew himself up; he sighed; he took one of her hands from the rail upon which it rested, and raised it to his lips.

She lifted her eyebrows in a little stare of affectionate astonishment.

"*Dear* James!" she said.

Still holding her hand, he sighed again, but smilingly. "Alas! I'm getting on for sixty."

"Sixty's nothing," she replied in a warm, low voice. "Oh, no! We shan't be Darby and Joan for another fifteen years."

The gong for dressing had sounded some minutes ago. They turned and strolled towards the companion-way together.

All night the ship lay motionless but for the very slight heave of the swell. The absence of the customary noises and movements made everybody restless. Moreover, it was very hot. It might have been his imagination, but Sir James fancied that he could smell the land, and that the heat was a heat off the land, the heat of steaming forests. All night sheet-lightning flickered in the south and west. And the white light of the Atalaya lighthouse flashed monotonously. Sir James wondered whether the lights of the ship had been seen by anyone on shore besides the lighthouse men. Was the Salinas promontory quite desolate? Failing to sleep, he began to long for the dawn, when he would go up on deck and see what that hidden shore was like.

In the meantime, he could not stop thinking about Marion Oswestry. Should he ask her to marry him? It was improbable that she would refuse. She was assuredly as fond of him as he was of her. Would she not welcome, as he would, the added intimacy and constant, instead of intermittent, companionship? From the worldly point of view, too, each was in the position to give the other something. He had won his spurs in political, diplomatic, and literary fields; he was, quite distinctly, a figure in the world.

It was in his power greatly to assist Hugo. On the other hand, Lady Oswestry had money. To command so easily all the good things, all the comforts, that money could buy would, he reflected, be rather pleasant. As he grew older and went out less he would stand in gathering need of *home* comforts. And although dear Marion was really quite over-rich, she carried her excessive wealth so well that he didn't mind it; nor would he in the least mind being beholden to her for all the luxuries by which he would be surrounded. Why didn't he marry her then? Well! he wasn't quite sure. . . . He wasn't yet quite satisfied that. . . . But, perhaps, by the end of this cruise he would know.

The dawn was faint and exquisite. A colour that lay somewhere between pink and gold filtered slowly into the greys and blues of the mist. The horizon shrank away until in the south a low, vague coastline of trees became visible, a smudge between the hazy sky and the rippling water. Then the sun struck brilliantly upon the white of the lighthouse.

Sir James and Hugo, in their pyjamas, were on deck watching. They saw the little pilot-boat approach, throwing the sparks of its wood fires out of the funnel. They saw the "*pratico da barra*" jump off the boat into a canoe; and the canoe, paddled by three natives nude to the waist, was alongside in five minutes.

Everyone came on deck early that day. The white *Clio* was now gliding through a water which became thicker and yellower. Along the south only was a shore-line visible. Field-glasses revealed an occasional village with a few stone houses rising from among a litter of palm-leaf hovels. Swampy islands, suffocated with vegetation, struggled up here and there out of the yellow swirl.

Although there was very little to look at, Simpson was busy as showman. "Mud and water?" he kept repeating with a wide flourish of his arm. "Mud and water! Thousands of miles of it—an expanse larger than European Russia—all mud and water."

"And a few trees," put in Hugo.

"Oh yes. Plenty of trees—sticking out of mud and water."

The young women began giggling behind Simpson's back. "Mud and water!" the little man went on; and after an hour or so nearly everyone began playing bridge.

Mary was not among the bridge players, but she had been on deck quite early, and although looking pale, her air was quite cheerful. That night she had been through a crisis; her anguish had burnt itself out. She had ceased to be the subject, she had become the contemplator, of her misery. And of her love, too. She couldn't go on entertaining so much love and so much misery; she hadn't the strength. If anything happened to Gerald she would kill herself; but in the meantime she would be happy.

Then, later in the morning, she received another wireless through the Para station. Gerald, now on the *Mauretania*, announced he had been offered an important part in a new film play which was being manufactured in New York. He asked whether he should accept or whether he should stick to his Havana plan. Mary flushed deep with anger as she read the news. "Idiot!" said she, speaking out loud. She crumpled the sheet up, threw it into the corner of her cabin and began furiously brushing her hair. "Fancy asking me which to do!" she thought. "Whether to make a fool of himself as a beautiful young hero in some vulgar, stupid film or to kill himself in a hydroplane chasing the *Clio* about the West Indies." For the first time in her life she saw Gerald with unflattering clearness. In the war his foolhardiness had been under the direction of other minds, and all had been well. He had become an ace. But left to himself, what would he ever achieve? Even of follies he was incapable, she suspected, of carrying out any but the simplest. Concentration of mind, common sense, foresight, imagination—of these he possessed not a particle.

She stopped, aghast at her disloyalty. She looked at Gerald's photograph and her eyes grew misty. Was she doing him an injustice? Well! it was being put to the proof. If he stopped in New York and fell in love with a cinema star, that would be the end. And if he killed himself, that again would be the end. She wasn't going to advise him which to do. She would wait and see.

When she appeared on deck again Lady Oswestry drew her aside and said: "Mary, darling, did you sleep better last night? Tell me truly." Whereupon she hugged her hostess with fervour, exclaiming: "Dearest Aunt Marion, you mustn't worry about me any more! Really you mustn't! I'm perfectly well and happy. I only wish I didn't feel such a pig for not having enjoyed everything before. But now I'm going to. I'm going to simply love it all!" And certainly for the remainder of the day her spirits never flagged.

On the other hand, Stella that morning was inclined to be thoughtful. For one thing it was absurd, she reflected, that no mention of the fact that her husband was at Para should pass between her and Lady Oswestry. Accordingly, seizing upon an opportunity when they were standing together scanning the distant shore, she said in the voice of utter boredom which was not uncommon with her :

"I wonder if I shall see Jock at Para."

"Who's Jock?" inquired Lady Oswestry, glancing round with a certain surprise.

Stella's field-glasses were raised to her eyes. "Oh, look!" she exclaimed. "Look at all those coppery natives on that strip of beach. One can see them quite clearly. Jock," she went on in a casual tone; "he's my husband, you know."

"My dear! Is he at Para? Why didn't you. . . . But how exciting! Do you suppose he knows you're coming?"

"She's innocent!" said Stella to herself. She had no doubt about her hostess's sincerity. But was it possible that Lady Oswestry ignored the fact that Jock drank and that she was fed up with him?

"Jock drinks and I'm fed up with him," she said, uttering the words that went through her mind.

"Yes," said the other quietly. "I had been told he drank." She paused in hesitation, then went on : "But I didn't know your husband was at Para, my dear, or I should have spoken to you about it. Perhaps you would rather not see him? I don't see why you and he should run up against one another.

THE *CLIO*

Of course he may hear that you are on board the *Clio*, but——" And she broke off, her eyes questioning.

Stella sighed impatiently. "I don't know——" she muttered. Then, evidently feeling herself ungracious, she put out a hand. "I'm sorry," she hurried on, "because, if Jock turns up, he might be rather a bore. I haven't seen him for two years, and what he's like now I really can't imagine."

As the sun's strength increased new vapours were drawn up out of the humid forest, and the distance was dimmed by a thicker haze. But at noon the white towers of Para Cathedral became visible, and an hour later the *Clio* was in port. Luncheon was a restless meal, and presently everyone was hanging over the rail staring at a harbour which was no more interesting than any other harbour in the world. Portuguese officials swarmed over the vessel. The chattering was tremendous.

"In these parts," observed Sir James, "the trouble is that they won't take bribes. Their mentality is too low. Only the more intelligent of the higher functionaries are bribable. The others have been hypnotised by Red Tape. Look at that little man with the protruding eyes, and a bunch of pink, blue and yellow forms in his hand. His whole body is quivering with excitement. That is because he is afraid that a pink form ought to have been used instead of a yellow one. The matter doesn't touch him personally of course. He won't, in any case, get into trouble about it; and he knows that. Yet his passion is nearly suffocating him. Look at his gesticulations! Look at the sweat pouring down his face! How is a man like that to be bribed? If you pressed a thousand-dollar bill into his hand he would throw it to the ground and spit and dance on it. No, no! His whole soul is tortured, racked, devastated by the question whether Captain Wilson did right or wrong in filling in a yellow form instead of a pink one. It matters terribly to him although he couldn't for the life of him say why."

" We are none of us very different from him really," said Veeder, the engineer, who was sucking blissfully at one of Sir James's cigars.

The latter had found out long ago that Veeder was of a philosophic turn of mind. So this comment did not astonish him; but he prepared to disagree with it.

"It appears to me," he began judicially, "that *some* of us *are* very different. The things we get excited about are, I think, more important things; although of course we couldn't very well explain *why* we get excited about them, or even *why* they are important. But we can point to European civilisation and say to that man: " People like you couldn't have built it up, and couldn't even keep it going although we have shown you the way!"

" Yes, that's all right, sir," returned Veeder. " That's all right, but——" A call from the captain interrupted him, so with an " Excuse me, Sir James," he hurried off.

Chapter 6

A LITTLE later the whole party, led by Harry, were trooping along the quay. The men were in white from head to foot, the women's light, soft colours were those of a spring nosegay. They moved along a background of booths out of the dark mouths of which came the rich smell of smoked rubber. Not many people were about, for the hour of siesta was hardly over. Harry stopped at the corner of a street running inland and surveyed his following with majestic good-humour. His behaviour since he set foot on land had amazed everybody excepting perhaps his mother and Hugo. From his air one would imagine that of all the port officials he was the lord and chief. Customs officers, passport officers, dock superintendents and policemen, one and all found him their master in the arts of vociferation and gesticulation. Portuguese flowed from him in a nasal torrent. He twirled his cane at them, slapped them on the back, poked them in the stomach, and even expectorated over their shoulders. This last demonstration of blood brotherhood won their hearts; he was ready, they could see, to kiss them all on both cheeks, if necessary. But it was not necessary. They let him and his party through one barrier after another in record time, waiving their rights of search and fumigation.

"And now," said Harry, "where shall I take you first? The main shopping streets, eh? The Joao Alfredo and then San Antonio before the crowd there gets too thick. And we'll wind up with one of Ribeiro's best drinks at the dear old Da Paz."

There was a polite murmur of acquiescence. Hugo glanced at his mother and then bent his head to examine his white shoes. The smile on Lady Oswestry's face was enigmatic.

"Lead on, Harry dear!" she said.

They moved up the street, a bright and noticeable company. Outside the cafés swarthy gentlemen of every age from fourteen onwards, sat and stared. Heavens, how they stared! The young women of the *Clio*, accustomed to pretending to be quite unconscious of masculine regards, felt that this time they were really up against it. To one another they were obliged, after a few moments, to confess that the gallantry of the Paraense beat everything hitherto experienced. It was like walking through a barrage. The bright air was darkened by the fumes of smouldering passion.

Harry was immensely imposing, leisurely, and jocular. Where the street San Antonio was narrowest and most crowded, he would stand in the middle of the way and let the tram bear down upon him with its clanging bell until the house fronts re-echoed to the shrieks of warning. Then to the purple-faced, frenzied conductor he would raise his hat with a gesture of such regal magnificence as to stop the man's maledictions and impose a universal hush.

The whole party, a little dizzy, a little breathless, took refuge after a while under some palms in the

centre of a white, gleaming, but dirty square. Here
it was possible to open one's parasol and take breath,
and even to make one's voice heard. The people
sauntering by were chiefly black, white, brown,
citron, café-au-lait, and puce in colour. Harry
informed the company that bar-tenders, engine
drivers and dentists could be told at a glance by the
enormous Brazilian sapphire rings which they wore
on their middle fingers. State functionaries could
be distinguished by the uniform of a tight frock-coat
and bowler hat; the worthy bourgeois always wore
a heavy gold chain across his white waistcoat, and
boots of a peculiar yellowish-green kid. "Picturesque
eh?" said he. "All damn picturesque!"

"I suppose," said Olga to Hugo, "Harry knows
Para very well."

Hugo grinned. "He's never been anywhere near
South America before in his life."

"What?" cried Olga, staring.

"What?" echoed Stella, who was standing by.

Hugo enjoyed their astonishment. He had been
watching them watch Harry. And although Harry
had made him a little uncomfortable once or twice,
on the whole he had been amused. The relations
between Harry and Olga in particular tickled him.
About a year ago Harry had made love to Olga;
it was probable that Olga was daily expecting him
to make love to her again; and it was possible that
she was even prepared to marry him. Harry's
oddities, therefore, were a matter of some concern,
and even of some, pain, to her. "Oh dear! Oh
dear!" she was thinking. "Can I ever marry a
man who behaves like that?" But she was very

careful to hide these feelings. She pretended to understand Harry perfectly and to be intensely entertained by all he said and did. " Darling, just look at him now ! Isn't he *too* delicious ! " She had gurgled these words over and over again whilst watching Harry's antics in the customs house. And in the streets of Para her flaunting demeanour seemed almost to be an imitation of Harry's. But a certain brazenness of manner did in truth come naturally to Olga. She could stand still in the street and point her parasol at a stout, powdered woman of the Para aristocracy and scream with laughter without meaning any harm. It did not occur to her that the good lady's feelings were perhaps more easy to hurt than those of a fish in an aquarium.

Hugo was shrewd enough to understand Olga pretty well, and Harry he understood enough to know that Olga provided him with a slightly malicious amusement. But that didn't mean that Harry might not marry Olga some day. Hugo's idea of Harry was that he was an absolutely undauntable *farceur*, a born comedian, actuated by an intense vanity—a man who would do anything for the sake of an effect. What else there might be in Harry he didn't know. As regards Olga, although he had no intention of marrying her herself, he was somewhat piqued by the preference which she showed for Harry. The fact was that during this voyage he had fallen a little under the influence of Olga's physical attractions. He wouldn't admit it, but it was so. He couldn't help following her about with his eyes. Her big well-built body appealed to him. He couldn't help thinking about her when he was with

Stella, and this not only spoilt his pleasure in Stella, but also made him feel slightly ashamed. For Stella, he knew, was—in a kind of way—in love with him. Besides, he admired Stella's mind and character. Not only had she twice as much intellect as any other young woman he knew, but she was absolutely honest—honest with herself—and generous-spirited.

The thought that his mother was no longer ignorant of their relations gave him, on the whole, satisfaction. He disliked having secrets from her. She still occupied a place in his heart high above that of any other woman. The desire to do her credit was at the root of his ambition. It had always angered him to see Harry refusing to lend himself to her schemes. He knew that in spite of disappointments her love for Harry continued undiminished. Perhaps he was a little jealous of his elder brother. Undoubtedly certain traits in Harry's character annoyed him. In particular his interest in other people's affairs. Harry was a born *intrigant*. Nothing escaped him; he kept a note-book, and his notes were in a secret code. The kind of thing that exasperated Hugo was this. One day in London he suggested that a few friends should be summoned to a small impromptu dance. " Humph ! " had said Harry, consulting his note-book. " I should wait a day or two if I were you."—" Why ? "—" Because, as it happens, Hugo me lad, three out of your four best gals won't be feeling quite in form to-morrow evening."

And now Hugo was about to receive another illustration of Harry's peculiar turn of mind. Whilst they were resting on the benches in the square a man, who had evidently been looking for them, came running up. He was hot, flustered, and full of apologies. Hugo guessed that this must be Schmidt, the manager of the banana plantation. He was a stumpy fellow with a shaven bullet head, and the expression of a bully although his manner was servile. Harry rose rather hastily and drew him aside; but not before Hugo had overheard something which astonished him.

"I think I have been successful; I have done everything possible; but Mr. Barlow is not an easy man to——"

The rest of Mr. Schmidt's sentence was inaudible, but those few words had been enough to set Hugo off along a line of puzzled, angry speculation. What the devil had Harry to do with Stella's husband, Jock Barlow?

The question fretted him. It introduced the suspicion that his mother was Harry's accomplice—that she had, in fact, lied to Stella a few hours ago. But after a minute he dismissed that suspicion and was able to thrust the matter aside—at least for the time being.

Like everyone else that afternoon he was feeling enervated by the heat and not a little bewildered by the novelty of the tropical scene. In the forefront of his mind was the picture of a very long iced drink. This preoccupation, as the talk showed, was shared by all. Everybody was *dying* for a comfortable deck-chair in the shade with an electric fan at one elbow and an immense tumbler at the other.

It made him distinctly uncomfortable, however, to feel that Harry was interesting himself in the question

of his relations with Stella. That question was
complicated enough without Harry's butting in.
It was a moral question; and Hugo had a strong
moral sense. The problem whether he *ought* to
marry Stella worried him considerably. Would his
mother mind much? Would Mr. Barlow much mind
dying? Or rather, to put this a little differently,
was Mr. Barlow worth making an effort to save?
Would it be wrong to allow him, for Stella's sake,
to drink himself quietly to death? Was it even
Stella's duty to return to her husband whether he
went on drinking or not? And in the event of
Harry's trying to bring this reconciliation about,
ought he to oppose Harry? Orthodox morality
would seem to say that he ought not. But the
ethical point was complicated for Hugo by the fact
he wouldn't really feel much temptation to oppose
Harry. He wasn't, unfortunately, very keen on
marrying Stella. And the unavowable reason for
this was that his desires had already, in great measure,
transferred themselves from Stella to Olga. Would
it be fair in these circumstances to marry Stella?
Yes; because his desire for Olga was, he felt sure,
impermanent. It would cease so soon as her sturdy,
but well-shaped legs ceased to be waved every day
under his nose.

This last reflection was made somewhat bitterly,
as he was sitting opposite Olga on deck the next
morning. Olga was reclining on a very low chair
and looking already rather flushed and demoralised
by the heat. Her lids had dropped; when she
raised them it was to observe Hugo staring at her
knees with a queer angry concentration. After a

few seconds of intense self-consciousness on both sides, Olga twitched her skirt down and closed her eyes again.

Heavens! how hot it was! The sun made nothing of the awning overhead. And the damp! It soaked all the energy out of you. Hugo asked himself whether Olga was really asleep or only pretending? And what would she say if he were to get up and kiss her?

These thoughts were interrupted by the sound of a renewed outburst of discussion on the other side of the deck. Should they go up the Amazon or should they not? Lady Oswestry had conflicting sentiments. Jane, who had been ransacking Para, had found one—only one, alas, but still one!—pot of her special face cream. And that would last a fortnight, or perhaps with frugality three weeks. . . .

Olga rose and joined the group. Her vote was for going on. She had the spirit of adventure. Besides, obsessed by the dread of getting fat, she was reflecting that a fortnight's Turkish bath was bound to reduce her waist and hip measurements. And who could tell what effect these tropical days might not have on Harry—or Hugo?

Angela, too, was in favour of going on. Life on the *Clio* amused her. Gossip on board ship is apt to become more intimate and detailed than anywhere else. And then the tropics! The sleeping on decks in hammocks, the opportunities for being seen *en deshabille* (there was no one on board whose lingerie was as amusing as hers) oh, and all the little wickednesses which hatch out in a moist atmosphere of between eighty-five and ninety degrees.

As for the others, they finally expressed themselves in favour of continuing the voyage—all except the captain, who was sulky, and Harry, who kept silence.

Before long it was decided that the *Clio* should proceed as far as Manaos, a three or four days' journey up the river. A big map was produced, and it was a surprise to many to observe that Para could hardly be said to be situated on the Amazon proper. To get into the main stream which flowed north of the Island of Marajo, one had first to cross the wide sheet of water known as the Bay of Marajo, and then make a tortuous passage northward along the water-lanes between the island and the mainland.

While the map was being studied the heat increased, and suddenly a quite remarkable smell enveloped the whole ship. Lady Oswestry, who was very sensitive to smells, dashed down to her cabin, but not before imploring Harry that their stay in Para should be as brief as possible.

It was at dawn two days later that the *Clio* steamed out of the harbour and round the *Ilha de Onças* into the estuary which at that point was more than twelve miles across. By the time her passengers were up and about she was in the midst of a dreary expanse of yellow-green waters, broken into short waves by a north-easterly breeze. The sky was overcast and hung very low. The southern shore was visible as a long streak of deeper blue on the grey-blue haze of the horizon. In the north the coast line of Marajo was only to be glimpsed at intervals when the mist thinned out. The whole scene had a curiously bleak and chilly aspect. But for the hot damp feel of the air one might have imagined oneself in the Thames estuary.

Angela, Mary and Olga were sitting together in the saloon. Angela was stitching at an elegant and flimsy article of underwear; Mary was writing letters in her desultory, slapdash fashion; Olga was knitting a heavy, woollen muffler destined for a fisherman in the North Sea. During these last days the three girls had sought each others' company more than usual. They were moved by an impulse which worked upon something more profound than the differences of temperament and character which separated them. Each, of course, was well accustomed to admiration; that she was desirable and desired was to each a running accompaniment to her existence, like a soft strain of music, a condition of which she might, or might not, be taking notice, but which played as important a part in her life as the possession of a secure income, or even as the enjoyment of her five senses. But that these young women were nubile and attractive was a fact that the gallant citizens of Para had lately brought into unusual prominence. And this linked them together in an enhanced consciousness that they were all three experiencing life from an uncommon, a privileged, standpoint—the standpoint of a pretty girl.

The link might be impersonal but it counted for a good deal. Just as Mary might have formed a devoted friendship with a deaf or a blind girl, so she could and did make friends with girls devoid of physical charm; those alliances, however, were not established upon so profound a basis as that, for instance, underlying her rather ill-compounded friendship with Angela.

For she *was* a friend of Angela's; she had made Angela's acquaintance at Miss Smith's fashionable school, and had been a stout defender of hers when the girls whispered together that the reason why Angela's stay had been cut short was that her parents had been asked to take her away. Meeting her in London later, she had been seized with admiration for Angela's independence and immunity from scruple. Mary's conscience led her an awful life. She found she had a passionate inclination towards those things of which her conscience disapproved. She was tempted to flirt outrageously, and in particular with married men, because they were not in the position to spoil everything by asking for your hand. She loved expensive things, and late hours, and dangerous sports—such as flying with Gerald. These propensities distressed her father and mother, and their remonstrances made her furious; although, unfortunately, her wretched conscience was on her parents' side. But for her conscience and an instinctive affection which she was unable to overcome, she could have treated her parents as cavalierly as Angela did hers. But although her reason insisted that her parents were not particularly lovable, and that there was nothing really wrong in the pleasures which she craved, she could not follow her natural bent in the calm, comfortable, strong-minded fashion that Angela did. So she thought of herself as lamentably weak-willed, and envied Angela her strength of character.

For her part Angela regarded Mary with feelings

that were at once admiring and derisive. Mary's troubles seemed to her quite insubstantial. Life is simple enough, thought Angela, if one has money. All *she* complained of—and, alas, it was a big grievance —was the poverty of her parents. Had they been of low birth as well as poor she would have utterly renounced them long ago. But having endowed her with a good name and allowing her, as they regretfully did, perfect liberty, they had their uses. For Angela was not by any means one of your mannish, self-supporting young women. On the contrary she was frivolously feminine. She had a passion for dress. And this was part of a wider interest, the dominating—one might almost say the exclusive— interest of her life, her regard for appearances. Her appreciation of the finer shades in the art of modes and manners was swift and unerring. Although without a spark of true æsthetic taste she not only knew how to dress to perfection, but she could divine what her set, the smart pseudo-Bohemian group, would select for admiration from among the latest books and pictures. To do her justice, however, among her intimates she didn't keep up the pretence of caring one jot about any form of art. She was unashamed of her emptiness because she couldn't honestly believe that any of the things people made such a fuss about—religion, science, art, philosophy— had anything in them. Nor—to be quite candid— did she see anything in love. She combined a complete physical frigidity with a complete lack of any moral sense. What she did see was that it was as important to display the right tastes and opinions as the right manners and clothes. There was dowdiness and smartness. And who ever wanted to be dowdy ? If it was part of the game to pretend that other standards existed, one didn't of course *believe* it in one's heart. And yet, the funny thing was that sometimes it paid to be simple. Take Mary as an instance. Although a simpleton, she was not in the least dowdy. She had a kind of natural distinction; she escaped dowdiness in the very way that some children do. Nothing was so smart, reflected Angela, as certain kinds of naïveté.

Chapter 7

THE three girls agreed that there had been a certain enchantment in the languorous atmosphere of Para. In the halcyon days of rubber it had made a fugitive pretence of being a little Paris, but now in all but the very centre of the town a perpetual siesta reigned. In the new suburbs that had intended to be smart, grass was sprouting on the ledges of the hairdresser's window, and the jungle looked in at the modiste's back door. It had been pleasant to wander in the wide, empty avenues of mangoes, to sit rocking oneself on the terrace of the Café da Paz, and in the evening to lean over the rail of the *Clio*, whence one could hear the night life under the trees of the central *praça* and watch the electric trams slipping along the water front, while every quarter of an hour there came a great boom from the bells of the cathedral behind. The charm of it was no less real for having been so largely dependent upon the mere air of the place. This medium drew notice to itself with a soft, constant insistence. It gave you, all the while, gentle caresses, assuring you that in all the world around nothing was cold, nothing chill, nothing would cause the faintest shrinking in the most supersensitive flesh. It was a perpetual pleasure to let this air touch and feel you. It was delicious to go for motor drives, letting it blow in under your clothes

—especially at dusk when it seemed to have even more "body" to it and to convey to you, even through the tactile sense, its rich, moist perfume.

Yes, they were quite sorry to leave Para; out here in mid-stream the view was desolate and the breeze might almost be called cold. Francis presently came in exaggeratedly rubbing his hands together and stamping with his feet.

"The doctor wants to know if you all took your quinine this morning. It's no use my telling him that his ideas are quite out of date. He still clings to quinine as a preventive." So saying he danced a kind of little hornpipe. He was evidently in fine fettle. "Sir Guy Nettleby—you know who I mean—well, he said to me himself just a day or two before we started——"

"Francis, for heaven's sake!" protested Mary. "How *can* I write letters, if——"

"But what's the point of writing letters now? Don't you realise we are going up to Manaos? There's nothing to be gained by——"

"I *will* write letters if I want to," returned Mary fiercely. "Go away!"

Francis went and sat down beside Angela.

"Something absolutely priceless to tell you," he murmured into her ear.

"Really?" They both glanced over at Olga who was barely within earshot. "Go on," continued Angela in a low voice, "but don't talk too loud."

"It's about Harry. I've kept it to myself for two days; but now I can't any longer."

Angela smiled faintly but eagerly.

"Didn't I," continued Francis, "always say that I suspected Harry——"

"Of what?"

"Oh, of being everything you can imagine."

"Well? And now?"

Francis chuckled and stuck a cigarette into his long amber holder.

"You remember our second evening in Para when everybody was by way of going to bed early, and I went into the town by myself: well, I wandered around for a bit; but I can't say it was very amusing; the lovely, powdered ladies with the black eyes——"

"Oh, hurry up!"

"So finally, at about one, I went back to the quay and was looking round for someone to take me over to the *Clio*, when suddenly—I caught sight of Harry! He had evidently just come on shore," continued Francis after a dramatic pause, "and as I caught sight of him he was setting out towards the old quarter, you know, behind the *Ver-o-peso*. I saw him, but he never saw me. And so I followed him."

Again Francis paused; then:

"My dear, he went up through a maze of narrow alleys and finally disappeared into the filthiest little restaurant I ever set eyes upon."

"Did you go in?"

"My dear, I wouldn't have gone in for anything in the world. Too many *bichos* in a place like that. —But I had a look through the window.—Oh, and I forgot to tell you, Harry was disguised!"

"No!"

"Yes! He had no crease in his trousers."

"Don't be silly. He wasn't really disguised, was he?"

"He had on a very old suit which I've never seen him in before. He was sitting at a table when I looked in——" And Francis broke off mysteriously.

"What were the other people in the place like?" asked Angela, glancing in Olga's direction. "Was he talking to anyone?"

Francis leaned closer and murmured something into her ear. Angela's face never changed; she remained bent over her stitching.

Jumping gaily to his feet, Francis fox-trotted with an imaginary partner round the saloon. Then, stopping again before Angela:

"What do you say to that, my dear?"

Angela darted another look at Olga beneath her lashes. It amused her to shock Olga, but Francis's manner suggested a little too much.

"Olga darling, our Francis is out-Francising himself this morning. I wish you'd take him off my hands."

Olga's lips curled and she made no reply.

"Well, I'm off," said Francis suddenly. "Mary, if you want to get some of that ink off your fingers before lunch I'll lend you a bit of pumice-stone. Oh, by the way, has anyone seen the professor this morning?"

At the mention of the professor a smile appeared on the girls' faces.

"Darling old duck!" said Mary. "I *am* glad we've got him on board."

Francis began laughing to himself reminiscently; still laughing he wheeled round and tripped out of the room.

At eleven o'clock the evening before an incident had taken place which resulted in the addition of two new members to the party. Mah-jong and bridge were going on in the saloon when the wire-gauze door against insects was gently pushed open and a grey-bearded, bespectacled old gentleman timidly looked in. It took him several moments to gain courage to enter, but at last he came forward and introduced himself as Professor Brown, the naturalist.

"My dear professor," exclaimed Harry, at once shaking him warmly by the hand, "I am delighted—more than delighted—to make your acquaintance." And the professor, who was beginning to apologise for his intrusion, found no time to get another word in.

"I noticed your name in the register of the Hotel da Paz," Harry went on. "If we had been staying longer at Para I should have mustered the courage to send my card up to you. For, let me tell you, I myself am an enthusiastic entomologist."

At this the professor's hand, which Harry was still clasping, renewed its cordial movement.

"I am delighted," exclaimed the newcomer. "An entomologist!"

"Oh, an amateur, an amateur!" said Harry with a gesture of lordly deprecation which sent Angela, Olga and Mary into the background to stifle their amusement.

"Might I inquire," continued Harry, "whether it was in search of lepidoptera——"

"That I came to Brazil?"

"And to the *Clio* this evening?"

"Not exactly," replied the professor, with grave suavity. "I want to explain. I am looking for a friend of mine who was to have sailed with me on the up-river boat to-morrow—Mr. Wilkinson.

"A Mr. Wilkinson," murmured Harry thoughtfully. "A clergyman?"

"No. Mr. Appleby Wilkinson. I dare say——"

"Why, of course!" put in Lady Oswestry, who was rather nervous as to what Harry was going to say next. "I remember reading some book of his once. Is it *that* Mr. Wilkinson, professor?"

The professor said it was. "I met him here a fortnight ago," he went on. "His company has afforded me great pleasure. We are staying at the same hotel. As you are probably aware, he has been sent on a travelling mission by the League for the Promotion of International Understandings."

"Really?" murmured Lady Oswestry politely. Her slightly mystified expression invited the professor to be more explicit.

"Mr. Wilkinson's mission is to study the diverse civilisations of the world. He will afterwards write a book elucidating the best points in each. The idea is that each should learn something from the others." And the professor sighed gently.

"You interest me very much," pronounced Harry in the manner of one determined to keep the conversation in his own hands. "And if I might throw in my opinion I should say that Mr. Wilkinson ought not to confine himself to the observation of *human* societies. As *you* know better than anyone, professor, there are other communities besides those of *homo sapiens*, which no student of terrestrial life can afford to overlook."

"My dear sir!" exclaimed the professor, his

lenses fairly scintillating with delight. "My dear sir! Is that not exactly what I have been endeavouring all these days to impress on Mr. Wilkinson. The colonies of the sauba-ant——"

"Vulgarly called the parasol-ant," interjected Harry, glancing round upon the others with a look of calm triumph.

"Exactly. Well, these colonies—as, after two years of continuous study, I am able to show—these colonies exhibit a social life and enjoy an efficiency of Government which are unequalled by any of our European States. I assure you that for complexity of organisation, differentiation of function, executive rectitude, scientific economy in administration and——"

"Professor!" cried Harry. "My own humble investigations have led me to identical conclusions. The rectitude of the official sauba-ant has always struck me particularly. Not once have I come across a case of bribery and corruption. Besides," he went on in a voice of indignation, "is it possible that Mr. Wilkinson does not appreciate the fact that these ants have had a system of proportional representation for the last fifty thousand years?"

The professor wagged his head smilingly at Harry. "This gentleman," said he, addressing Lady Oswestry, "has a charming sense of humour. He has almost made me forget my purpose. I came here in search of Mr. Wilkinson."

"Mr. Wilkinson!" murmured Harry. "True, true! He must be found. We will organise a search."

The professor looked rather surprised.

"Now"—and Harry rubbed his hands together—"how shall we proceed? Tell us when you first missed Mr. Wilkinson."

"Well," began the professor doubtfully, "it was, I should say, about an hour ago that he left the hotel."

"Ah-ha!" said Harry. "I see! He eluded your vigilance and slipped out of the hotel at about ten o'clock. I understand. I know how to plan this campaign. Hugo, I depute you to go and search the Moulin Rouge and that Casino place—what do they call it?—the *Bar Paraense*."

"Excuse me," began the professor, "but really——"

Harry interrupted with a knowing shake of the head. "Professor, don't be too sure! Very often the most unlikely——"

"But," cried the professor, "to name but one objection, Mr. Wilkinson was, I regret to say, slightly indisposed. He feared a touch of dysentry."

"Do *you* think it was dysentry?" asked Harry sceptically.

"Frankly, I do not. The symptoms were remarkably like those from which I myself suffered two years ago on first arriving at Para. And my symptoms —I confess it with shame—were produced by an over-indulgence in stewed turtle. I do not want to suggest," he went on hastily, "that Mr. Wilkinson was—what shall I say?—was in the least——"

"No, no!" put in Harry, "we quite understand. But the fact remains that Mr. Wilkinson was not quite well. Mr. Wilkinson had probably a slight touch of fever. Well, there is nothing like a touch of fever to predispose one to entertainment . . . to gaiety. . . ."

The professor turned to Lady Oswestry in a kind of despair. "My dear lady, my dear lady, I ventured to come on board your yacht because I have reason to believe that Mr. Wilkinson is *here*!"

Lady Oswestry smiled. "Here?"

The professor looked vaguely round the room.

"I assure you," said Lady Oswestry, still smiling, "he isn't here."

But the professor showed a singular obstinacy. Too courteous to argue, he insinuated gently: "Not in this saloon—but, perhaps, in the smoking-room?"

Lady Oswestry burst out laughing. "He's not on board the *Clio* at all, professor." And turning to the steward who was bringing in a tray of glasses: "Drummond," she said, "there's no one in the smoking-room, is there?"

"No, my lady."

"Nor on deck?"

"No, my lady."

"Has anyone come on board this evening besides this gentleman?"

"Not to my knowledge, my lady."

"There!" said Lady Oswestry turning again to the professor. "Do you still believe that I've kidnapped your Mr. Wilkinson?"

The professor sighed his gentle sigh and, going slowly to the door, beckoned to someone outside. A stolid Indian lad, clad in a white cotton coat and a pink cotton petticoat, came in. A few sentences passed between them in an unknown tongue, and a look of relief came into the professor's face.

"This is my servant," he explained. "And he says he has found Mr. Wilkinson."

"Ha!" said Harry. "Was he at the Moulin Rouge?"

The professor looked at the speaker reproachfully. "No," he replied. "Mr. Wilkinson is, as I said, on board."

There was a brief silence, broken only by little stifled sounds from the corner of the room where the young ladies of the party had congregated.

"Show him to me then!" cried Lady Oswestry impetuously. "Produce Mr. Wilkinson, professor! If Mr. Wilkinson is here—let me see him."

The professor inclined his head with courtly dignity. "José appears to know where he is. I will tell José to take us to him," he said; and he issued a brief order in the same foreign tongue.

A procession then set out on the discovery of Mr. Wilkinson. First, went the Indian leading the way, then the professor and Lady Oswestry, then Harry and Hugo, and the rest of the party could not resist the temptation to follow at a little distance. The Indian lad marched downstairs, and through the lower saloon, and along a passage, and did not stop until he reached the door of the gentleman's lavatory at which he pointed with a solemn finger.

Later on, the mystery of Mr. Wilkinson's presence on the yacht was very simply solved. The steamer by which he and the professor were to sail the next day, was scheduled to make so early a start that Mr. Wilkinson elected to spend the night on board. But as he was being rowed out to his ship a sudden spasm again overtook him; within a few yards was the *Clio* with her ladder almost within his grasp;

there was no one to see him board her—no one apparently about. A necessity which knew no law impelled him to prompt action; and he was fortunate, for in less than thirty seconds and without meeting anyone he found sanctuary. The Indian boatman to whom all ships were alike, and all the actions of white men equally inexplicable, had rowed quietly back to the wharf where, as luck would have it, he came upon the professor. The latter upon questioning him had been greatly mystified. Had Mr. Wilkinson made a mistake and boarded the *Clio* under the impression that it was the river steamer? Mr. Wilkinson was a very impractical man; and Mr. Wilkinson was not well that evening; Mr. Wilkinson probably had a touch of fever. The professor felt perturbed; to find Mr. Wilkinson and get him safely to bed on board the *Esperança* presented itself to him as his obvious duty.

Such was the incident to which the hospitable mistress of the *Clio* owed the presence of her two further guests, for she had insisted that the professor and the invalid should make their journey to Manaos with the advantages of the better food and better medical attendance that her ship could afford. Moreover, everyone on board already loved the professor. He was, as Mary had said, "a darling old duck." As for Mr. Wilkinson, he had not yet been seen; and there was much speculation as to what he would be like.

That gentleman (invested with a peculiar prestige of which he was quite unaware) did not, however, make his appearance on deck until four o'clock the next day. He revealed himself as a rather sallow, sparsely-

haired man of about fifty, whose stooping shoulders,
furrowed cheeks and brooding eyes proclaimed him
at once a member of the intelligentzia. He seemed
somewhat shy, or rather mistrustful, of the
people amongst whom he found himself. It was
noticeable that he addressed his conversation by
preference to the doctor, whom he had already seen
professionally; or to Lady Oswestry, to whom, as
his hostess, politeness was due. During tea his
eyes rested once or twice with wonder upon the
professor who, in the midst of a smiling and attentive
bevy of girls, was discoursing blissfully and quite
unself-consciously, upon the domestic habits of the
sauba-ant. For Mr. Wilkinson, on his side, was
terribly self-conscious. And his self-consciousness
was of that unfortunate kind which is impregnated
with class-consciousness.

"I should think," Sir James afterwards remarked
to Lady Oswestry, "there is probably no society on
earth imbued with a stronger class-consciousness
than University society. Dons, dons' wives and
dons' daughters speak a language of their own. They
have their own little reserved amiabilities, little dry
jokes, and little eloquent taciturnities, which the
outside world can't understand at all. To represent
them as forming an envious, unfriendly community is
signally unjust. The fact is that they are only happy
among themselves."

"Oh, yes," smiled Lady Oswestry. "I'm sure
that Mr. Wilkinson is very nice really. He'll get
less uncomfortable later on."

"I doubt it," returned Sir James. "He's not
prepared to like anybody here. He doesn't like our

manners. He doesn't like anybody to be unself-conscious—or at any rate to seem unself-conscious. All ease of manner affects him as showiness. In his society they all *pretend* to be shy even when they aren't."

Lady Oswestry still smiled.

"I *know*," said Sir James, "because I have a lot of friends at the Universities. When I go there I look uncomfortable; I shrink and mutter and wriggle like Mr. Wilkinson, and they like me for it."

But there were other reasons as well for the new-comer's mistrustful aloofness. Mr. Wilkinson disliked and disapproved of wealth; even when allied to an ancient name, it was not entirely acquitted of the taint of vulgarity. Being a good Liberal, he shrank from wealth just as, being also a man of letters, he shuddered before any symptom of a defective education. Wishful indeed he was to get on with his fellow-passengers, but in education they struck him as being much below the level of the wives and daughters of his fellow-dons. Not that he demanded highbrow conversation, but the University flippancy, the University jokes, to which he was accustomed, sprang from a more richly nourished, a more intellectual subsoil.

Chapter 8

FOR most of the afternoon the *Clio* steamed along the darkly wooded coast of Marajo. About an hour before sunset the anchor was dropped off the little town of Breves. The captain preferred not to undertake the next part of the journey by night, the waterways trending northward into the main stream being in places exceedingly narrow. Boats were lowered for a trip ashore, but at the last minute the doctor intervened.

"I have been talking to the pilot," he said. "I gather that Breves is full of malaria, and at sundown the mosquitoes will be coming out."

There was disappointment at this. At the distance of a quarter of a mile Breves looked idyllic. Its little white houses, and its big white church, all glowing in the evening light, cast charming reflections upon the water which was unruffled by any breath of wind. Many of the trees about the town were brilliant with red and purple blossoms. In the background there towered up the green wall of the forest.

The doctor called to the pilot. "Hear what Señor Joao da Pinto Cunha has to say."

Señor Joao presented the face and figure of an ill-shaved, intemperate, unsuccessful Napoleon. His only tongue was Portuguese, but behind him came his son, Joachim, who was prepared to be affable and voluble in any language under the sun.

"These ladies want to hear about Breves," said the doctor, after the formalities of introduction were over. Señor Joao grunted vaguely, inclined himself, and turned with a peremptory gesture to his son.

"Yes, yes. Very nice, very nice," said the latter. "Plenty peoples there once, but now nearly all gone to Antonio Lemos." And he pointed farther along the coast. While speaking Joachim kept his face fixed in a perpetual smile of politeness and punctuated his sentences with little bows.

"Why did the people move away from Breves?" asked Lady Oswestry.

"Because, my lady, most peoples die at Breves," replied Joachim, still smiling his smile of courteous gaiety. "Much *carapanas*, much malaria at Breves, so the Governor he build new city, fine city, Antonio Lemos."

"*Carapanas* are mosquitoes," the doctor explained.

"Is Antonio Lemos far away? And is it as pretty as Breves?" Lady Oswestry went on.

"Yes, my lady, quite near," returned Joachim eagerly. "Little way down Tajapuru. But peoples there now all dead. Fine cemetery. Big! I show him to you. Yes?"

Lady Oswestry gave a little frown and a laugh. "No, thank you. But why did the poor people at Antonio Lemos die?"

"Poor people?" repeated Joachim, catching confusedly at the words. "Yes, yes. Poor people—

seringueiros—no money—savages—pouah ! " And he made a grimace of disdain.

" But why did they die in their nice new town ? " persisted Lady Oswestry.

" Why they die ? Oh, my lady, the *carapanas !* the *carapanas !* "

" Are there *carapanas* at Antonio Lemos too ? "

Joachim laughed—a laugh of exquisitely balanced merriment and politeness. " Oh, my lady, hundred times more than at Breves ! Shall I take you to Breves, no ? Well ! to-morrow I take you to Antonio Lemos. Ah," he went on with the air of a genial host, " here comes crocodile man. He show you baby crocodile. Very pretty, very nice. You put him on your table."

Leaning over the rail, he pointed to a canoe which had just slipped up alongside without a sound. As they were looking down at the half-caste and his mysterious bundle of cargo, the doctor explained that this part of the Amazon delta was peculiarly unhealthy. Lady Oswestry's guests need not fear that their liberty would be so restricted farther on.

Meanwhile the man in the canoe was languidly preparing to carry his bundles up on deck. His emaciated limbs were covered by a thin cotton jacket and trousers. The shallow canoe rocked to his slow movements. He seemed very tired. All around and behind him the water lay smooth and glassy, reflecting the pinkish shades which were beginning to steal into the sky. The air had the softness of warm velvet ; and how soundless the whole scene was ! Thick trees dropped in a tangle over the complicated shore-line of inlets and promontories ; and the trees looked as if not a leaf of them had ever, ever stirred. The pilot and his son stood back talking desultorily in a low, nasal Portuguese. One felt suddenly as if one had been in the place for years. It felt like a place that is utterly tired of itself. Yes, unquestionably time hung heavy over Breves.

The crocodile man proved far less interesting than they had hoped. His wares consisted of little baskets and mats of plaited palm-leaf fibre, diadems of parrot and toucan feathers, arrows (the points of which were said to be poisoned with the famous curare), swords fashioned out of a wood that was almost as hard and heavy as metal, wooden drums, and, lastly, stuffed infant alligators. These had a depressing effect upon everyone. They were eight or nine inches long; they stood on their hind legs and tails, holding out their little forearms upon which you could hang your rings, or support a pencil, or fix a box for postage stamps or perhaps a small tray.

"The alligators' eggs," said the professor, "are collected and hatched in baskets filled with vegetable débris. The infant alligators are then confined in tubs of water and killed within a day or two. Among tourists," he added with a sigh, "the demand for these ornaments is considerable."

After the departure of the pedlar the silent stagnancy of the scene became still more oppressive. Everyone stared and stared at Breves, and Breves gave no sign. At last a feeling began to steal over the company that Bond Street was, indeed, remote. The big map was once again produced, and this time the professor was the spokesman.

"As you see," he said, "we are now about two hundred and fifty miles from the Atlantic, but a large part of the delta still lies before us. To-morrow we shall thread our way through an immense jungle-covered swamp intersected by narrow channels. This part of the world is veritably antediluvian. It presents a picture of what the earth was like before man came into being; of the time when the plesiosaurus and other gigantic lizards roamed, and the forests which now provide us with our coal sprouted out of the warm silt. Every year great floods sweep down the Amazon covering thousands of square miles with muddy water. Most of the country through which we shall pass on our way up to Manaos is inundated for at least two or three months of the year. In the Upper Amazon the water rises as much as fifty feet; here there is a variation of over twenty feet. Just now the river is almost at its lowest. The rises and falls which we observe here are caused by the tides. It is a curious fact that in the channels of this region the water flows sometimes one way, sometimes another. The great estuary up which we have been steaming all day is little more than a backwater of the main stream of the Amazon, which flows north of Marajo. There the current fights with the Atlantic tides and creates a dangerous bore. Three waves which are sometimes as much as twelve feet high rush up the river, sweeping over the low islands with devastating force. No one lives in those parts; nor would anyone live in this region were it not for the rubber-yielding trees and vines. This part of the earth is not yet ready to be the abode of man."

Everyone was interested; but, reflected Mr. Wilkinson, everyone ought to have known all this before. Later, as he was pacing with the professor, he said:

"I never cease to be surprised at the rarity of intellectual curiosity in man. I was just now talking to the captain and that little fellow Simpson. The captain was entirely without interest in any aspect of this country, while the only question that Simpson was ready to discuss was the future of the timber industry—and that of course strictly from the point of view of the dividend-hunter."

After dinner that evening, however, Mr. Wilkinson received an agreeable surprise. He found that Angela was prepared to talk to him about the latest—the very latest—pictures and books. What stimulated Angela to this effort was the fact that Olga had just been doing her utmost with Mr. Wilkinson without the least success. She had rather rashly confessed to a certain admiration for Mr. Stephen McKenna, had hastily tried to retrieve this by professing an even greater admiration for Miss Sheila Kaye-Smith, Mr. Thomas Hardy, and Mr. Eden Phillpotts, and then had done for herself by asking Mr. Wilkinson what he thought of *The Green Hat*.

The Green Hat had cast a sickly shade over Mr. Wilkinson's countenance, whilst he muttered something polite and inarticulate. Nevertheless, as Lady Oswestry had already noticed, he was doing his level best not to find them all stupid. When a remark was addressed to him he paused in the obvious effort to give it its least inept interpretation, and very often he answered as if you had said something

much more intelligent than what you actually did
say. For instance, Mary, wishing to break a longish
silence, had observed: " Isn't it extraordinary what
a lot of forest there is here ! " And Mr. Wilkinson,
after a desperate twisting of the fingers, had replied :
" Yes, I believe the variety of trees *is* unequalled
anywhere in the tropics. I am told that in little
more than one acre of ground you may find as many
as one hundred different species."

But Angela (though he doubted whether her knowledge was very profound) seemed at any rate well
informed on the subject of modern art. She was
voluble about Piccasso, Pruna, Dobson, Maillol,
Giraudoux, Soupault, and others of whom he had not
yet heard. She asked him whether he took in
Le Disque Vert, and said she had found that *l'Ane
d'Or* often had good articles on modern Spanish
literature. When he began talking about Don
Quixote she shied off; she was successful in con-
cealing the fact that her only reading since the age
of thirteen had been a fortnightly fashion paper,
which took pride in the intellectual as well as the
bodily equipment of its subscribers. It was great
fun. And having entirely eclipsed Olga, she got up
and drifted gracefully away.

The next morning at nine o'clock the *Clio* whistled
her farewell to Breves, steamed slowly past the
creeper-covered ruins of Antonio Lemos, and entered
a *furo* that very soon narrowed until it was no wider
than the Thames at Windsor. For most of the way
bushes and trees linked together by lianas rose
straight up out of the water, forming two dense
green walls. Occasionally patches of reeds and

aquatic grass appeared; here and there banks of mud thrust their brown shoulders out of the stream; and sometimes smaller channels branching off from the main *furo* presented gloomy mud-floored tunnels in the vegetation.

As the sun rose the heat became intense. The party on the *Clio* leaned over the rail and stared. There was very little conversation; not much presented itself for comment. One could not look *into* the forest because its outer skin of greenery was too thick. Only once in a while, where a big tree had recently fallen, a gap of darkness appeared. These gaps, especially when they were half-filled with smaller trees, gave one a measure of the great height to which the real giants towered. Stella and Hugo who had gone out into the bows, were astonished, when they looked back over the ship, to see how she had shrunk. In the great wide ocean she still kept her size; here she was a little white tub, the tops of her funnels being on a level with what looked like low bushes on the bank.

The monotony of this slow advance over the dark glassy water was broken at noon by the sudden appearance of a canoe with a solitary paddler who pushed out into the stream and hailed the ship. Joao and Joachim, who were taking turns at the wheel, replied excitedly; the engines were stopped, and a long shouted conversation in the mongrel idiom known as *lingoa geral* ensued.

It became known at last that a few miles farther on the channel was blocked. A couple of tall trees had crashed down at a point where the waterway had already been narrowed by mudbanks, so that it would be difficult, if not impossible, for the *Clio* to get past. It was accordingly decided to go back a short distance and cut across to another channel which ran in the desired direction. Captain Wilson's mien was tragic. In the privacy of his cabin he unbosomed himself to Veeder and Simpson. Joao and Joachim, he said, were, even as Dagoes went, brainless. He was ready to bet his bottom dollar that they had already lost their way—and perhaps it was just as well, for the sooner the ship ran aground the better. Better be stuck here than in the swirling current of the Amazon where timbers ten feet in diameter came down on you like battering-rams.

Meanwhile the *Clio* was gently backing down like a motor-car in a narrow alley, and no one but Captain Wilson was in the least perturbed. But when they saw the water-lane up which Señor Joao was intending to take them, even the ladies gasped. "It's going to be a tight fit, isn't it?" observed Lady Oswestry mildly.

"It's the depth I'm unhappy about," replied Sir James. "It doesn't look as if it *could* be deep enough. However," he went on cheerily, "I'm told that what is called the *repiqueta* occurs in about three weeks' time; and that means a five or six foot rise in the water. With the help of the *repiqueta* we shall no doubt get away."

While these remarks were being exchanged, the doctor was sauntering up to Hugo and Stella. They noted the twinkle in his eye.

"Well, doctor—is the *Clio* going to manage it?"

"Oh, yes, I think so," he replied easily. "I think Joao knows what he is doing."

"Then what are you chuckling about?"

"I've just found out something." And he continued after a pause: "Do you promise not to pass it on?"

They promised.

"Well, old Joao let out to me a few minutes ago that the route we've been taking isn't the usual route at all. We branched off from the Tajapuru very soon after starting. Joachim is responsible. He took the first trick at the wheel while old Joao was still snoring in his hammock. Joachim thought he would show off his wonderful knowledge of these waterways by taking a short cut."

Meanwhile the *Clio* was shuffling gingerly round into her new path, and in a few moments the forest on each side of her was so close that you could almost touch it with your hand. A tangle of lianas suspended from an overhanging tree actually caught in the aerials of the wireless and threatened for a moment to do damage. It was now easy to discern the shape of the leaves and the texture of the bark of the unfamiliar trees that moved slowly past. Not one was like any tree that Stella had ever seen before. They seemed to her to be intentionally outlandish, deliberately *bizarre*. And in the dead calm of the air they stood up with a motionlessness that was uncanny. She realised suddenly that English trees nearly always had a rustle or a shiver in them. They stirred, they whispered familiarly; they didn't stand staring at you like a snake ready to spring. Nor were they, like these greedy creatures, murderously competitive. These trees were sucking up the ooze and spreading under the sunlight with a sinister concentration.

When Hugo and Stella joined the rest of the party they found Joachim there holding forth in his cheeriest and politest manner. Never had his opinion of himself been better than it was now; a sheer fluke had put him on the right road again, and Joachim always counted sheer flukes to his credit.

"You like this *furo*—yes? Very pretty—yes? No peoples come this way. Only me. I know all *furos* here—hundreds, yes."

Chapter 9

AT four in the afternoon they came to a singularly beautiful spot. An effort had recently been made to clear away the jungle for a cocoa plantation; over a space of perhaps two acres the trees had been felled and in part removed. Then, as a few charred stumps still showed, the ground had been fired to rid it of undergrowth. But that labour was spent in vain; for the enterprise had been abandoned, and now the jungle was creeping back. Among the ashes on the ground there already blossomed orchid-like violet peas, and a blood-red passion flower whose buds looked like strings of tiny Chinese lanterns. Prostrate vines decorated the tree-stumps with festoons of brilliant blossom. Huge white convolvuluses hung from the surrounding boughs.

These details were plainly visible from the deck of the *Clio*, and they awoke in Lady Oswestry so sharp a desire to set foot on shore that she ordered the engines to be stopped and two boats to be put out.

The boats had to row back for a few hundred yards along the waterway, the dark surface of which shone with a metallic glitter under the sun. Wherever it was possible they kept under the shade of over-arching foliage. Mary put up her hand and tried to break off one of the hanging lianas upon which

there grew a delicate ivory fungus. She failed, for
the fibre was tough, and upon her parasol there
came a faint patter, as of falling raindrops. The
professor gently took the parasol from her and shook
it over the water. "I think those were ants," he
said, "and some of the ants here bite rather——"

A small shriek from Stella interrupted him, and
she exhibited two bright red patches on her forearm.

"Dear, dear! I think those must have been fire-
ants. They are very painful, as I well know. And
if I were you," he went on hastily, "I wouldn't
trail my fingers in the water. There might be some
piranhas about."

"Oh, Lord!" said Stella. "I don't know what
piranhas are, but if they are as bad as fire-ants——"

"They are much worse," said the professor, smiling.
"They are the only animal in this region that I'm
really nervous about. I once had a terrible experience
with them."

He was begged to narrate it.

"Well," he began, although with a certain unwillingness, "I was on a little expedition down the
Tocantins in a sailing-boat. I landed on an island
one day from a canoe with two natives, and when
we came back to the spot where the canoe had been
tied up, it had disappeared. The rope had been
bitten through by some animal—what animal I
can't imagine; I have never heard of such a thing
happening before. After a time we spied the canoe
drifting along about three hundred yards down-
stream. It was necessary to swim for it, but neither
of my Indians seemed to relish the idea, and their
unwillingness puzzled me, for there were practically

no alligators in those parts. At last one of them, after washing himself in a puddle, slipped very quietly into the water and swam rapidly off. But after he had gone about a quarter of the distance, to my surprise he turned back. I was just asking the other Indian about it, when the swimmer gave a howl and I saw a look of agony come into his face. At the same time I noticed that the water about him was rippled as by a shoal of fish; and then suddenly I remembered what I had heard about the piranha and my heart turned cold. That poor Indian lifted an arm to which I saw about half a dozen of those horrible little monsters clinging by their teeth. Then he went down and I never saw him again. His companion explained to me what must have happened. In swimming he must have scratched one of his limbs against a snag, causing a slight flow of blood. Knowing his danger he had at once turned back—but too late. For the slightest taint of blood turns the piranha into a veritable demon."

After they had landed Lady Oswestry inquired somewhat nervously about snakes.

"Oh, you needn't worry," said the doctor, strolling up. "I've got a lancet, permanganate of potash, and whisky, all ready in the boat."

"The number of poisonous snakes," added the professor reassuringly, "is very small compared to the great variety and abundance of harmless ones. Moreover, you can always distinguish a poison-snake by the shape of his head."

The whole party was now standing in a group on the bank. Longing eyes were cast over the flower-strewn carpet before them, but no one moved.

"Why didn't you tell us to put on gaiters?" said Lady Oswestry reproachfully.

The professor struck his forehead in self-reproach. "Ah, yes! the *carrapatos*. But they are not likely to be found here at this season."

"Is that a very bad kind of snake?" inquired Mary.

The professor smiled. "My dear young lady, you may put the fear of snakes out of your mind, I assure you. You have merely to look where you place your feet, and abstain from thrusting your hands into hollow tree-trunks, and no evil will befall. The *carrapatos* are less easy to avoid. *Carrapatos* are a kind of tick."

"Good Lord! I don't think I like this country," said Stella in an aside to Hugo.

"If you feel nervous," continued the professor, beaming upon the ladies benignly, "I shall be only too happy, upon our return, to examine your legs. With a little piece of cotton-wool soaked in tobacco juice I guarantee to remove every single *carrapato*."

The company had come ashore at a small landing-stage composed of half a dozen rotten planks which were slippery with lichen. From it a faint and narrow track extended inland. Along this the ladies now proceeded, while the men of the party showed their courage by tramping amid the flowering vines. Every few yards the professor stopped to direct attention to some plant or insect. But of the latter the butterflies alone aroused any enthusiasm in his audience. Huge blue butterflies of marvellous sheen fluttered nearly all the way before them. "These," said the professor, "are *Morpho Menelaus;* far less common is *Morpho Rhetenor*, whose wings are of a still more magnificent blue."

The track, after meandering diagonally across the clearing, plunged under the heavy vaulting of the forest.

"I won't go on," said Lady Oswestry decidedly. "I've been stung on the shoulder by some animal; and my legs already feel as if they required your attention, professor."

"So do mine," said Olga, who was bending down to scratch.

"If you feel a tickling," replied the professor, "the cause of it is most likely to be *mucuims*, tiny red creatures, very like our 'harvesters' at home." "The best way to treat *them* is with camphorated alcohol or petrol," said the doctor. "If you, gentlemen, wish to push on a little, I will take the ladies back."

The professor, followed by Sir James, Mr. Wilkinson, and Hugo, accordingly stepped on into the cool damp gloom of the trees. Hugo had been told to expect a bitter, rank smell of decaying vegetation, but the odour which actually assailed his nostrils was that of bad fish.

"I think we must be not far from the hut of some seringueiro," said the professor over his shoulder.

He was right. Three hundred yards farther on they came out upon a tiny clearing which ran in a strip along a narrow creek. The creek might have been fifteen yards across, but shallow, amber-coloured water filled no more than three yards of it. The rest was brown mud. In the places where the sunlight had fallen upon it this mud was covered by a kind of skin.

At the back of the clearing was a wooden cabin which looked as if it had been put together with the decayed remnants of a larger building, and on each side of it were palm-leaf shelters. Two or three children were playing about in front. Their skin was of a light brown colour, proclaiming them mamelucos, a cross between Portuguese and native. They were clad in cotton shirts. Under the shelter two women, one of whom looked like a pure Indian, were engaged in some household task.

The visitors were not tempted to approach because the ground about the dwellings was littered with fragments of fish,—the source of the smell which they had already noticed. As they walked slowly along the creek the women came out and stood in the sun staring at them. But their interest did not last long. Presently the Indian woman came down with a jug which she dipped into the water; she took no trouble to avoid stirring up the mud; but she was fastidious enough to pick out of the jug some small creature which she had scooped up with the water.

The party moved on. Their attention was engaged by a man whom they observed wading in the liquid mud a little further towards the mouth of the creek. He carried a net not unlike a landing-net, but he was not using it. He was using his hands instead; every now and then he bent down and grabbed at something just under the mud. As they watched him he brought up a small fish which he transfixed upon a pointed stick where several others were feebly flapping.

There was something hypnotic about the silence and loneliness of the place. They stood watching the fisherman without any sense of the passage of time. The first to rouse himself from this torpor was Mr. Wilkinson, who began to fidget, and then made a resolute move homewards. The others followed, but with a kind of reluctance. The creek itself was now in shadow, but the sun still threw a golden bloom of light over the upper half of the great billowing trees that walled it in.

The short passage under the forest seemed even darker and danker than before, but when they came out into the flowery space beyond, they found it as brilliant and beautiful as ever in the mellow evening light. In spite of this, however, it no longer attracted them. They lay under a dreamy depression and remained silent until they reached the boat. As they rowed back the professor discoursed about the different kinds of mudfish to be found in these parts. Many of them, he declared, were by no means bad eating. But the habit of drinking stagnant unfiltered water was to be deplored. Moreover, that mameluco family was living on an unhealthy spot and in typically unhealthy conditions. "The children, I fear, are already suffering from ankylostoma."

Mr. Wilkinson made no reply, but Hugo asked what ankylostoma was and how the professor had been able to make a diagnosis at that distance.

"I noticed that they were eating earth," was the answer. "And that morbid craving is a sign of the presence of an intestinal parasite."

"Oh," said Hugo, and relapsed into silence.

On the *Clio* tea was in progress, accompanied by a lively chatter which fell pleasantly upon their ears. In the centre of the table was a vase filled with the flowers that had been picked. Everyone was there except Olga, who appeared a little later looking very fresh in a new white dress.

"I had two *carrapatos* on me," she announced triumphantly.

"Oh, my dear, where?"

"At the back of the knee."

"Who found them?" asked Angela.

During tea the conversation turned upon the dwellers on the creek, and in the sociological discussion that followed Mr. Wilkinson's latent contentiousness made itself felt. Not that he said very much, but his expression and manner were eloquent. So eloquent were they that Sir James could not forbear to stir the hidden fires by saying:

"In my old age I find myself utterly devoid of humanitarian principles and with my humanitarian sentiments much weakened. As a young man I believed in the Government of the people, for the people, and by the people. That belief has died a natural death. I now believe only in Government by the rich for the preservation of our existing culture and civilisation."

Mr. Wilkinson turned to Hugo with a somewhat supercilious smile. "What do you say to that?" he inquired, not doubting that youth would be on his side.

"Well," replied Hugo with diffidence, "I can't help thinking that democratic systems have shown themselves to be unworkable in principle; and, what is more, that the underlying ideas are now being shown up as unsound."

"Ethically unsound?" inquired Mr. Wilkinson.

"Ethically unsound," replied Hugo with firmness.

Mr. Wilkinson compressed his lips. That a new class of youthful reactionary had arisen was not unknown to him; but he had not yet come into contact with it. Here was a specimen that would be worth his study. He surmised that Hugo had fallen under Sir James's influence, and he resolved to counteract it as vigorously as he could.

In his judgment of Sir James he failed to allow for the fact that the sympathies of the latter went out to his like, whilst his own were bestowed most readily upon the creatures who stood at the farthest remove from himself. Thus his sentiment offered itself in the first place to animals, next to savages, then to the lowest ranks of civilised society, and so on up the hierarchy of intellect until he came to his own class and kind who, godlike, were able to dispense with sympathy.

To those who stood above him in the *social* scale he was, as a rule, indulgent, as he took it for granted that they stood beneath him intellectually. Had Sir James been less intelligent, he would have regarded him with more leniency. He would, in fact, have taken pride in being able to get on with him. For he liked to think that he could converse as man to man with coal-heavers, shopkeepers, and even dukes. Indeed, it pleased him to count a sporting duke amongst his friends, to say nothing of a peer interested only in jewellery, and a few county families whose

countiness pigeon-holed them as effectively as a
black skin would have done—or a naïve admiration
for the best seller. Just as the shoemaker should
stick to his last, so, he considered, should the aristocracy stick to their stupidity.

After a while he got up and fell to pacing the
deck in company with Stella and Hugo. During a
discussion upon social reform he tried to make up
his mind whether Hugo was or was not superior and
supercilious—a young man lacking in the generous
impulses proper to youth. Hugo, on his side, could
see that he was under judgment, and he kept hoping
that Stella would put Mr. Wilkinson on the right
track, for he felt unable to do so himself. But to
his surprise and annoyance Stella did just the
opposite. She contrived with skilful malice to make
him seem just what Mr. Wilkinson thought he was.
After a time poor Hugo began to wonder: " Does
Stella really think me a superior, supercilious young
man ? " And in the end he even asked himself:
" Can it be that I actually *am* one ? "

Life seemed very difficult. He wondered with pain
why Stella took pleasure in annoying him. Although
his own sentiment for her was cooling, he could not
contemplate with any composure the idea of her
tiring of him. Besides, what had he done to make
her feel positively unfriendly ?

She was his first mistress. The liaison, although
not highly romantic in colouring, had meant a good
deal to him. It had begun only a few months ago,
and he was already asking himself how much longer
it would last. A short life, an early natural death—
alas ! that was unbecoming history for a love affair.

One might reasonably question whether Stella and he had ever been really in love.

As a matter of fact Stella had taken him because she felt the need of a lover, and of all her men friends Hugo had been the best qualified for the position. Then, being a young woman of temperament, she had fallen under the spell of his attractions—but unwillingly, for that subjugation injured her self-respect. Whilst conceding to Hugo qualities of mind which she lacked, she regarded him as on the whole her intellectual inferior. And if she was weak enough to be proud of her lover's wealth and birth, she was also contemptuous of her own snobbishness. Moreover, although she did not misunderstand Hugo's character, as Mr. Wilkinson did, his political creed was offensive to her. The sentiment which she ruled out of her love affairs she put into her politics. She was a sentimental revolutionary.

When Hugo advanced the propositions (1) that men were by nature averse from all effort, especially intellectual effort, (2) that science by increasing the complexity of civilisation made it not less, but more, onerous, and that there was no good reason for believing that matters would ever be otherwise, (3) that in these circumstances it was difficult to see how civilisation could be maintained except under the severest pressure of competition reinforced by the dread of destitution, (4) that the miseries of civilisation were, however, probably not greater than those of barbarism, and (5) that the highest, not the greatest, happiness of the greatest number was the end that should be kept in view—when she and Hugo argued these points she generally got the worst of it. But she remained, as was natural, completely unshaken in her hatred of the present scheme of things and firm in her desire to shatter it to bits.

Presently, as they stood looking at the sunset, Harry joined them, and this set Hugo off along another line of troubled speculation. Stella had confided to him that she, too, had overheard Schmidt's words concerning her husband. And she had requested that the matter should be left in her hands, declaring with some show of anger that she intended to have it out with Harry herself.

That was three days ago, but so far she had done nothing. Nor had her manner to Harry changed in the slightest degree. Indeed, as they all four stood chatting together, Hugo observed that she gave more attention to Harry than to either Mr. Wilkinson or himself. A gloom spread over him which matched the gathering gloom of the landscape. The two towering walls of forest were intensely dark. Overhead a strip of pink sky shone palely, and its colour was reflected in the glassy water of the *furo*. But that pink was not gay. No, that pink only added to the melancholy of the hour. A sense of mystery crept over Hugo's spirit. Human beings and forests and sunsets were all part of a sad and insoluble mystery.

He looked round for Sir James, who was in some ways the least mysterious person on board. But twenty minutes ago the latter had disappeared into the smoking-room to join the genial Mr. Simpson over a whisky and soda. Hugo, glancing in, saw them laughing together, and with a sigh he took himself off to dress for dinner.

Chapter 10

A LITTLE later Sir James strolled down the companionway. He was feeling at peace with the world. Life, he reflected, was on the whole very pleasant. The intellect and the senses in combination opened up such a variety of diversions. If the elements were few and simple enough, the combinations and permutations were almost infinite. There was even a new pleasure to be derived from the old things by viewing them from a fresh angle. Not only were Einstein and jazz music and Freud and Diaghileff entertaining, but Lucretius, Shakespeare and Mozart gave one a novel sensation nowadays. Women, too—they delighted one differently. For instance, here was Marion's French maid coming down the passage; in his callow youth his pleasure in her trim figure would have been a hungry pleasure—a pleasure impaired by a number of fierce inward conflicts. But now—no conflicts! He was master of the situation. An instinct told him just what he might, without loss of dignity or risk of future trouble, do. He smiled at her as she came along, and when she pressed herself against the side of the narrow passage to let him pass, and lowered her eyes and plucked at her ridiculous little apron, he did not kiss her. No! For he had not been so taken up by her attractions as to fail to notice that Angela was peeping from behind her curtain. So Marie passed unkissed.

As he went on light footfalls sounded behind him. Exactly! Here was Angela in exquisite going-to-the-bathroom attire. He took her by the arm and revolved her to get an all-round view. "Charming!" he pronounced. "Charming!"

The temptation to do nothing but let one's eyes rest appreciatively upon the women of the party, and take iced drinks and cool baths was, he realised, becoming overpowering. How long, he asked himself, how long would Mr. Wilkinson keep his moral and intellectual energies unimpaired? His own in the course of the last twenty-five years had not exactly atrophied—he wouldn't admit that—but without question they were less vehement. "One takes not only oneself but other human beings so much less seriously than when one was young. Human relationships seemed then so momentous. And yet," he went on to himself, "when I come to think of it, even as a young man my desire was to keep my amours light and superficial. I have always been in search of the frivolous—I might almost say—of the vulgar. How is it, then, that nearly all my liaisons have been grave affairs in which there has been a real contact of personalities?" And he sighed.

Less than ever now did he want to take up any new responsibilities, hamper his freedom, or even enter into a relation of give and take. He didn't want either to give or to receive sympathy; he didn't want any close contact of any kind. "Well! —how, then, can I marry Marion?" The question embarrassed him seriously. He knew women well enough to realise that in marriage Marion would demand *something* more than what he was now giving as a friend, who saw her on an average once a week.

There was the physical side of the marriage, too. But she was fifty, he close on sixty—so that need hardly be taken as a major issue. And yet . . . .

In the course of retrospection he had come to realise that all his life he had hunted after an abstraction, —the abstract female, devoid of all personality, the woman without a mind, without a character, the creature with whom you could not make any mental contact whatsoever. The lure of the woman you passed in the street resided in the fact that whilst physically present to your eyes she offered mentally a blank. And when you imagined yourself with her it was not as the giver and receiver of irrelevant impressions—no, you imagined yourself with a creature whose psychical existence was nothing more than the counterpart of her visible allurements. You endowed the woman with a new order of being, with a life restricted to the requirements of your desire.

Charming women, women of character, culture and refinement, had been willing to marry him, but he had not wanted them. The stinging rebuff of his life had been administered by a girl whom he knew to be his inferior. And the sting of that rebuff came from his knowledge that in rejecting him she had followed just those finer instincts which he in selecting her had betrayed. She had possessed neither money nor position, and, young as she was, her reputation was already tarnished. She had had everything to gain from marrying him, and she had accepted his offer. But at the last minute she had run away with a journalist, a common, corrupt man of middle-age and indifferent health—but the man to whom she was drawn by a true affinity of character.

Smarting with shame, he had entered forthwith into a liaison with a woman, socially and culturally his equal, and in every other respect his superior. This woman loved him for what they had in common —for those qualities which he so inadequately prized. Her love was grounded upon a community of mind which was none the less real for his being so indifferent to it. " I never really loved her," he now said, looking at himself without illusion and without disgust. " In my case it is : ' *Deteriora peto, altiora sequor.*' "

As he was dressing there came a knock at his door and Harry lounged into the cabin. Harry was already dressed, and Sir James noticed, not for the first time, that Harry's hair and collar and shirt-front and shoes shone with a lustre unattainable by ordinary mortals. The gloss upon Harry, the perfection of his attire, would have been a sad vulgarity in anyone else ; but it suited him. It was the costume for the part, just as a red nose and big checks were proper to the old-time comedian.

Twitching up his trousers that were much too well creased, Harry seated himself upon the bed and mumbled out something that Sir James couldn't catch. The frogs outside were showing the visitors to their country what, under favourable circumstances, they could do. But Sir James had a notion that Harry's remark might have been interesting. So he put down his hairbrushes and closed both portholes.

"Not too late to stop your baldness from spreading," said Harry. "You should try my stuff—worth a guinea a bottle; and they charge you two."

Sir James was not only disappointed but slightly annoyed. His hair, for a man of his age, was abundant.

"Thank you, my dear boy." He spoke in a tone of appreciative interest. "You must give me the address."

"My birthday to-day," Harry went on, after a pause.

"No?" Sir James again seemed interested. "Well, you're still young enough not to mind——"

The fixing of his collar prevented the ending of the sentence.

"Going to celebrate it with special dance to-night. Chinese lanterns on deck—very pretty."

"What about the mosquitoes?"

"With luck shan't get any. We're just at the end of the *furo*. We'll be catching the breeze off the main river. But that's not what I came to say."

Sir James looked absent-minded. "It'll be pretty warm work dancing," he murmured.

"You know that little spec. you joined me in? What was it you said you'd put up?"

"Two thousand."

"I thought so. Well, I have to give you a cheque for six thousand three hundred and fifty odd. Not bad, eh?"

"Not at all bad," said Sir James, whose heart was

beating faster. "In fact, my dear Harry, you stagger me."

This was true, although the speaker's voice did not show it. "I'm richer by over three hundred a year," Sir James was thinking to himself. "And to me three hundred makes quite a difference."

"I'd rather you didn't mention this to anyone," said Harry carelessly.

"Not even to your mother?"

"No."

Sir James reflected.

"If I've made six thousand I wonder how much you've made," he said slowly.

Harry laughed. "Shan't tell you."

"All right." Smiling, he came up and shook Harry by the hand. "You know, I'm extremely obliged to you. Six thousand means something to me. Really—you're a marvel, Harry!"

A grin answered him. Then Harry said:

"The man you have to thank is Stanford. Damn him."

"How's that?"

"Or perhaps I should say Mary."

"Oh!"

"For making Stanford lose his head and play the giddy goat with all my messages."

"You mean—this big win was something of a fluke?"

"If Stanford had not messed up everything you'd have made five or six hundred and no more. I'm a bit of a gambler, I allow. But the things that fellow Stanford made me do—by mistake, mind you, by mistake—might have ruined a Rockefeller.

However, by the grace of God it's gone the other way."

"Harry," said Sir James, and he put his hand on his shoulder. "You won't go on any more now?"

"Don't need to," said Harry lightly. "Oh, no! Oh dear, no!"

They went slowly up on deck. Searchlights in the bows were casting a theatrical brilliance upon the forest. It was stage scenery that drifted by on either side—spectacular lianas, obviously cut out of cardboard, great buttressed tree-trunks that would sound hollow if you tapped them, fringes of aerial roots hanging by wires over your head, heavy masses of orchid cunningly suspended in mid-air; and all this slipped by endlessly, noiselessly, out of the inexhaustible darkness into the darkness again.

Said Harry with a flourish:

"Ladies and gentlemen, I myself will now mix you a refresher as I learnt it from the best bar-tender in the Eastern Seas. The juice of an orange, half sherry-glasses of gin and Italian vermouth, half liqueur glasses of maraschino and brandy, a couple of drops of peach, orange and angostura bitters; and shake the whole up with cracked ice."

Even Mr. Wilkinson took a refresher; and he took it not merely to show that he was no pussyfoot. For the first time in his life he was possessed by a thirst which insisted that only an alcoholic beverage could satisfy it. The sensation, he reflected, was instructive; and the experience should help to widen his sympathies. For the same excellent reason he drank four glasses of champagne at dinner—and he felt better for them. Everybody drank a good deal. The doctor, the captain and Mr. Simpson, who were present on this occasion, put forward in concert a powerful argument in favour of moderate drinking. A friend of Mr. Simpson's, who kept a poultry farm, intoxicated his hens regularly twice a day, at lunch and at dinner, and thus obtained four times as many eggs. The doctor explained how this came about. The action of alcohol was to deaden the higher brain centres, thus inhibiting the flow of speculative thought in the hen and concentrating her energy within the lower centres which regulated the physical processes. Mr. Wilkinson felt some doubt whether it was morally justifiable to dim, in these lowly creatures, the light—a feeble one no doubt—of their higher psychical activities; but he said nothing.

The dinner was really wonderful. European foods had been banished almost entirely from the menu. There was a soup of dried *pirarucu*; fried *mandii*, a small scaleless fish which growls when caught in the net; roast *Pomba trocal*, a kind of wood pigeon; turtle steaks, cooked in a slightly astringent sauce; *sorbets* of *cupuassu* and *mamao* served with manioc cakes; and as a savoury, *bichos de taquara*. This last dish was sampled by Stella by way of experiment, by Mr. Wilkinson from a sense of duty, by Harry and the professor from curiosity. The last two alone knew what these strange little objects, looking like tiny fried bananas, were. When the last mouthfuls had been consumed Harry informed the company that they were large grubs, found in the nuts of certain palm trees, and cooked in the native fashion which was to grill them over a hot fire after carefully removing the heads and entrails. It was a curious fact that the grubs, cooked whole, caused a kind of dreamy intoxication similar to that of opium.

In the centre of the table was a veritable mound of fruits and nuts of which everybody felt constrained to taste at least three or four kinds. Dinner went on in a desultory fashion for nearly two hours.

A warm, black, velvety night enclosed the *Clio*, which was now gliding slowly, very slowly, along the southern bank. The other bank had receded and was scarcely to be discerned. Bats, some small, some very large, flickered in and out of visibility; the lights in the bows and the Chinese lanterns overhead were besieged by enormous moths. Here, too, in far greater abundance than at Para were the fire-flies.

"I shall be disappointed," said Harry, "if we don't come across the species which have red and green lights. The green lights shine from the eyes and the red one is in its proper position at the tail. Am I not right, professor?"

The professor admitted that Harry was very nearly right. Certain kinds of fire-flies were able to emit at will white, red, or green lights from their eyes.

Presently a very creditable jazz band recruited from the crew struck up a familiar tune, and without a moment's delay several couples took the floor. The attempt not to get hot was utterly abandoned.

"Have you noticed," said Francis to Angela, "the *urubu* is looking quite cheerful to-night?"

The *urubu* was their name for Mr. Wilkinson, who

was perhaps a little like the baldheaded, stooping, rather mournful vulture who sits upon the roof-trees of Para.

"Yes. And look, my dear! Stella's trying to get him to dance."

"He'll be sick if he does. He ate three of Harry's grubs before he knew what they were."

"Mr. Wilkinson!" called out Angela in passing. "I never knew you were a dancer! If he asks me," she went on, "I'll sit out and talk literature."

Francis giggled. "I told him before dinner that your favourite occupation was being a mannequin—I said you started as a manicurist, but found the work too brainy."

"You didn't! Well, if you did, I'll tell everybody that you——"

"S'sh." Francis, genuinely alarmed, did not wait to hear what the impeachment would be. "My dear, we really can't afford to turn catty now. We've got to live together for another three weeks, remember. Have you decided about Hugo and Stella?"

"Yes. Hugo's too good. He knows his mama wouldn't like it. Not that Stella isn't ready."

"My dear, there's simply nothing that Stella wouldn't do. They say she was Lenin's mistress for one day. It's on the strength of that that she wrote her book about him."

"I'm longing to see her husband. I believe he's simply terrific!"

"Oh, I forgot to tell you. That night at Para when I went to the Moulin Rouge I met a man who knew him. Drinks like a fish, he said, was kicked

out of the Consular service for stealing gramophone
records, killed three natives one day, since when
none of the best people have asked him out, and——"

A pinch from Angela stopped him. Glancing over
his shoulder, he saw that Stella and Mr. Wilkinson
were just behind. Mr. Wilkinson would have acquitted
himself not badly had he realised that for modern
dancing one's partner must not be held at arm's
length. His endeavours to keep Stella at what he
considered the proper distance resulted in a kind of
wrestling match; for Stella was quite determined
to give instruction to Mr. Wilkinson whom she
regarded as a pupil, and the closer she hugged him
the more violently did Mr. Wilkinson struggle to
keep her away. In a few minutes Stella was obstinate
and angry, whilst poor Mr. Wilkinson thought he
was in the grip of a nymphomaniac.

"What is the matter with those two?" asked
Sir James, viewing them with some astonishment.

"Stella's giving him a lesson," returned Hugo.

"Obviously. The lesson of his life," murmured
Sir James. "But what has he done to deserve
it?"

The best dancers by far were Harry and his mother,
and they danced together for most of the evening.
Sir James could not ignore a light smart of jealousy
as he watched them gliding about over the deck.
Good, but in a different style, was Francis, whose
little feet flipped about with steps borrowed from
the clog-dancer. Hugo divided his time between
Stella, Mary and Olga, with great impartiality.
While he was dancing with Mary, Angela said to
Olga:

"Isn't your cabin next to Sir James's?"

"Yes." Olga was sucking orangeade through a straw. When the last drop had gurgled up, "Why?" she inquired.

Angela gave a little smile and said nothing.

"Look at Francis! Isn't he comic?" was her next remark. "And do you know, my dear, the way this climate is making his hair come out is simply awful. If you take a little of it between your finger and thumb and pull, it *all* comes out— and practically without his feeling it—just like a big white cat we had at home. But it makes him furious. Do try it."

Olga looked at her companion coldly.

"I do love Francis," Angela went on. "He's in pyjamas now because he wants to look manly. But, do you know, he wears a nightgown in London. He calls it an old-fashioned nightshirt, but really it's just like a girl's nightgown. I do adore Francis."

Olga was ruminating over the proximity of Sir James's cabin to hers; at last the temptation to ask Angela what she meant became irresistible.

Angela looked down at the deck, smiling.

"I believe he's got a periscope," she said mysteriously.

"What *do* you mean? What should he do with a periscope? It's a thing the soldiers used in the trenches."

"Yes. It enables one to look round corners. And I'm told he looks out of his porthole and round into yours every night when you're undressing."

"I don't care if he does," replied Olga crossly, and she got up to dance with Mr. Simpson.

Angela's teasing annoyed her because Angela was one of the few people who knew that, although her manner with men was free and easy, at heart she was a veritable prude. And probably Angela guessed that she was afraid of men just because they attracted her. When a man took the initiative with any boldness, Olga's heart began to beat sledge-hammer blows, and despite her repeated resolutions to the contrary, in a few minutes she would fly. She suspected Angela, and rightly, of being as cool as a cucumber with men, and yet of being willing to go to almost any lengths with them.

On this particular evening Angela was feeling in the best of form. Her little cheeks had a faint unusual flush and, although her expression remained angelically serene, her eyes had an alertness at the back of them. She had already prevailed upon Hugo to kiss her, reduced to a jelly-like condition one of the crew, a big handsome young fellow of eighteen (whom in the darkness of the stern she had engaged in the task of showing her some new stars), and she had made Hugh Stanford entirely forget both Einstein and Mary for at least ten minutes.

But this didn't amount to much. She was capable of more serious work, and saw that this evening presented favourable conditions. Sir James, tired of watching Lady Oswestry and Harry, had tried a turn with her, and presently he had said: "My dear Angela, if anyone could give me the illusion that I was an accomplished fox-trotter, it would be you."

They chatted together a good deal that evening.

Angela saw that he was no less attracted for having summed her up pretty shrewdly. "What a sensible man!" she thought. "He knows that I'm neither virtuous, nor intellectual, nor romantic; and he doesn't mind!" From the beginning of the voyage she had had her eye on Sir James. And she was now confirmed in her opinion that she might do worse than marry him. Her reasons were as follows: (1) To marry at all was not easy. (2) He had a title, a position in Society, and a sufficiency of money. She was a little in need of social rehabilitation. This marriage would answer the purpose. (3) He would be far less exacting than a young man. He knew just how much he could expect of her. He would ask for no more than observance of the conventions. (4) She would look forward to becoming a well-set-up young widow before so very long.

Sir James on his side was amused. One or two recollections helped to give him a clue to what was in Angela's mind. He remembered, for instance, that about a week ago Hugh Stanford's news-sheet had contained the information that hematite pig-iron had gone up two shillings a ton; that the body of a young woman had been found in a Saratoga trunk in the Edgware Road; that Lord Beverley, aged seventy-six, had married Miss Mima Dudley, aged nineteen; that five hundred thousand Chinese had been drowned by a tidal wave; and that Miss Bébé Sanger of Los Angeles had insured her legs for seventeen million dollars. Of these items the only one that had interested the company was the news of Lord Beverley's marriage. "Sporting effort!" Francis had commented with gaiety. "Mima Dudley's frightfully pretty." Olga had remarked rather coldly that it would have been more suitable if he had married the girl's grandmother, and Angela had cried out: "Oh, no! Everybody would think that quite dull. It's much more amusing as it is. As Francis says, so *much* more sporting." And now, with the memory of this in his mind, Sir James murmured to himself: "I believe—I really do believe Angela wants *me* to be sporting."

Chapter 11

No one had any wish to go to bed that night, but the band could not be kept up for ever; so at last Lady Oswestry, supported by the doctor, drove the young women to their cabins, out of reach of the mosquitoes which were beginning to show some activity. The men gathered in the smoking-room. Even Mr. Wilkinson felt the need of a whisky and soda.

Presently Hugh Stanford came in and went up to Harry. "I'm very sorry, Lord Oswestry, I can't get any answer from Para."

"Oh, well!" And Harry blinked up at him through the smoke of his cigar. "I suppose we must expect that kind of thing."

"Why, sir?" asked Stanford with directness. "It seems to me odd."

"I don't think so," returned Harry; "I'll talk to you about it to-morrow. What South America needs," he continued, addressing the company in general, "is a Mussolini, a Diaz, or a Lenin at the head of each State. Do you know that the President of the Commercial Association at Manaos complained not long ago that marconigrams from Rio habitually reach him thirty days late? And what's more, the telegraph line between Para and Manaos never worked decently until 1911, when it was taken over by an English company."

"In my opinion," replied Mr. Wilkinson, whose hatred of despotism was intense, "material efficiency (which can, after all, be attained in other ways) is too dearly purchased at the price of a dictatorship."

"Diaz in Mexico, Lenin in Russia, Mussolini in Italy," murmured Harry musingly. "I am not sure that——" He broke off to glare at Hugh Stanford, who had not accepted his dismissal.

After a moment's silence the latter said: "Am I to report to the captain, Lord Oswestry?"

"No. The captain, as you know, is down with fever. You have reported to me. That is enough."

"Down with fever!" exclaimed Sir James. "At dinner he was livelier than I've ever seen him."

"Lively enough one minute and half dead the next; that's the way in this country," observed Harry cheerfully. "But the captain's fever wasn't caught here. He got malaria into his system seven years ago."

Hugh Stanford was still standing his ground. "I can't help thinking, Lord Oswestry, that something is up at Para."

Harry gathered himself together and rose slowly to his feet. "Something's up over most of the Amazon valley to-night," said he, pointing through the open door. "Come on. Let's brave the mosquitoes. One ought not to miss this."

He was right. Somewhere up the river an electric storm was in progress, and the display was now at its height. Sheet lightning kept up an almost continuous glare among the huge cumulous clouds lying across the western sky. Wonderful were the peaks and valleys of that aerial world made visible by the white fires that flickered about them.

"Damn it all!" said Harry, turning upon Stanford. "With a disturbance like this going on, how can you expect your little bits of machinery to work?"

After a few minutes on deck everyone, excepting Harry, went below. Harry remained pacing up and down as was his wont. Everything was now very quiet; the deck was deserted; the saloon lights were out. Alone the windows of the wheel-house and of the wireless office remained illuminated. Harry entered the wheel-house, exchanged a few words with Joao and tapped the barometer. Then he went to the wireless office where he found Hugh Stanford reading a book on the Quantum Theory.

Leaning against the open door, he surveyed Hugh with a friendly grin.

"Young feller," said he, "bring all wireless news direct to me. I'm censor for the present. Understand?"

Hugh's stare slowly changed into a smile. "Very well, Lord Oswestry."

Harry resumed his pacing. It was late—nearly three o'clock. Once or twice he veered towards the companion-way as if intending to turn in. But the night was the sultriest yet experienced, and Harry's eyes showed that he was still far from sleepy.

Although wide awake, however, he was deeply immersed in his own thoughts. He failed to notice Stella who had come up on deck. When at last he did catch sight of her he gave a distinct start.

They were standing at a distance of about five yards from one another. Stella's china-blue eyes rested upon him in a fixed stare.

"I thought of trying the meat-safe to-night," said she in an expressionless voice.

She was referring to a wire-gauze cage which had been constructed on deck. It had been fitted with three hammocks in case any of the ladies should prefer to sleep in the open air.

Harry passed his hand over his forehead. "Yes. Why not?"

There was a pause; then Stella came slowly forward. She was swathed in a pink silk wrapper and had bedroom slippers on her feet.

"Pretty warm to-night," observed Harry conversationally.

"Yes. Is that why you don't go to bed?" And she looked at him as if she resented his presence there.

Harry leaned back against the rail, tilted his face up, and said lazily:

"I was considering . . . the question of marriage."

Stella laughed.

"Olga's a nice girl, what?" Harry went on.

"Very."

Harry brought his chin down and looked at her. "Can't you answer a fellow seriously?"

"I'm quite serious," returned Stella with a touch of impatience. "Olga *is* a very nice girl."

"Better to marry a nice girl," mumbled Harry, "than a—not nice girl."

"Much better," returned Stella in a tone of withering contempt.

"Trouble is . . . I don't much care about girls," said Harry reflectively.

"That shows your good taste," replied Stella.

Harry thought this over. "You serious?" he asked.

"Quite sufficiently."

Harry grunted, and there was another long pause.

"I should like to ask you something," said Stella.

"Right."

"What have you and Mr. Schmidt got to do with my husband?"

"Oh!" Harry smoothed the hair at the back of his head.

"Well!" And Stella's blue eyes fixed him aggressively.

"Damn it!" ejaculated Harry after a silence. "Why shouldn't I do your husband a good turn if I want to?"

"But, pray, why should you want to?" inquired Stella disagreeably.

"I offered him a good position on a healthy little coconut island in the West Indies," returned Harry in an injured tone. "Good pay, plenty to do, and a few pleasant companions—who don't drink."

"Thank you," returned Stella with polite fury. "Very kind of you. . . . But why? Why? Really your passion for interfering in other people's business. . . ." She choked. "D'you think I don't know why you've done this?"

"Well, if you know. . . ." mumbled Harry.

"Let me tell you," said Stella, "that I wouldn't marry Hugo for anything in the world."

Harry looked pained.

"Hugo's quite a good sort," said he.

"Too cold-blooded for me!" said Stella. "Too infernally reasonable. I'm *not* a nice young woman, you see."

"No," said Harry, "you're too good for marriage. That's why it's just as well you should have a husband alive. Keep you from marrying again."

Stella snorted. "Oh! Free love is the thing for me, is it?"

"That's right. You've got brains. And now, look here!" He turned and faced her squarely. "I'll tell you a secret."

Stella laughed aloud, a laugh of scorn.

"I," whispered Harry with an air of mystery, "I have brains too—of a sort."

There was a longish silence, then:

"Oh, good night!" exclaimed Stella rudely, and walked away to her wire cage into which she disappeared, banging the door behind her.

Harry resumed his march up and down the deck. After a few minutes he approached the cage.

"Do I disturb you?" he asked.

"Yes," said Stella.

"Sorry. I'm going down now. Good night."

But he did not go down. He moved to the other end of the deck and stood peering into the darkness. The night was starless. Not a glimmer anywhere. The sheet lightning had ceased. One could tell from the faintness of the frogs' croaking that the *Clio* was at some distance from the shore. She was going at half-speed through the heavy soft obscurity; and the loneliness here seemed greater than in the middle of the Atlantic.

After leaning motionless against the rail for perhaps five minutes, Harry raised his head in the attitude of one listening. A faint hum, as of an aeroplane, was audible over the water. He frowned, puzzled. Nothing could have been less expected. But in a few moments his expression changed; a look of eagerness illuminated his face. Walking quickly to the stern he stood listening and staring.

It was not very long before a bright, but distant, light came into view. "A motor-boat. A racer!" murmured Harry, for the exhaust was now rattling like a machine-gun, whilst the light grew rapidly larger. "Must be going nearly forty miles an hour to overtake us like this!"

As the noise grew louder he looked round with a grin of slight uneasiness, then turned and made for the captain's quarters. The electricity had just been switched on in the bedroom. He drew back the curtain and put his head in at the window. "Hullo, skipper! I was afraid that row would disturb you. It's my man, Schmidt, I fancy. He said he was going up to Santarem. We shall see him there to-morrow, or he may call in on me now. But I wish he'd muffle his exhaust, damn him; he'll be rousing the whole ship."

The captain, who was sitting up in his bunk, sank back with a sleepy growl.

"Feeling better?" inquired Harry.

"Not much."

"You go off to bye-bye again." And Harry withdrew.

As if in answer to his wish the engine of the motor-boat had suddenly become silent. Harry went to the wheel-house and bade Joao go dead slow. The light at the stern was drawing nearer. Five minutes later a motor-boat was alongside. At Harry's orders a rope ladder was let down, up which instantly there climbed a young man dressed in white.

The stranger was of remarkable beauty. He resembled a youthful grandee of old Spain. His age could hardly have been more than twenty; his features were delicate but virile; the sinewy grace of his figure showed that he had not been bred in the tropics.

Smiling eagerly he advanced upon Harry and flinging his arms round his shoulders kissed him on both cheeks. "Success!" he cried in Portuguese. "Complete success!"

"But, my beloved Pedro, it shouldn't have come off till——"

"Bah! What matter!" exclaimed Pedro. "I will explain. It is well!"

Harry looked round about. There were no intruders upon their privacy. Alone out of the wheel-house Joao peered in astonishment. Harry thrust his arm through Pedro's and drew him well out of earshot.

There had been, however, another highly interested witness of this scene, and that was Stella. In her wire-gauze cage she was well concealed, but her view of Harry and his companion had been excellent. Leaning on one elbow she gazed after them as they walked away. The young stranger was talking rapidly. It was too annoying their moving away, and her not being able to understand Portuguese better. The incident struck her as beautifully romantic—in the true Conrad tradition.

For a quarter of an hour she had to wait, her mind working furiously the while; then, to her joy, the two men strolled back and halted within a few yards of her cage. Harry cast several glances in her direction, and as he was standing under a deck light she could see that his glances were expressive of a kind of interior amusement.

After a few moments he drew his companion still nearer, and then with the words: "Stand there, dear friend!" he himself stepped back three paces as if to take a snapshot. It was not, however, a kodak that he levelled at Pedro but a strong electric torch. The figure of the adolescent shone out against the black cave of the night—a bare head, a white shirt unbuttoned at the throat, white trousers and shoes. He might have been a young cricketer on an English field. His clothes looked English, but they were stained and crumpled. In his hand he held a gold cigarette case, from which he had been about to take a cigarette. Frowning smilingly at the glare, he asked:

"Harry! What joke is this?"

"No joke," replied Harry, switching off the light. "I wished to photograph your image upon my mind, beloved Pedro. It is now there, imperishable!"

The young man laughed and put his hand on Harry's shoulder.

"We part again. But not for long. And when we meet once more, my heart, it shall be as——"

"Hush! hush!" ejaculated Harry with admirable dramatic effect. And together they stepped forward to embrace. But Pedro spoilt the moment by drawing back to exclaim:

"*Jesus!* We are forgetting the gasolene!"

"No," said Harry; "I never forget anything. You'll find it already in your boat."

"Then farewell!" And Pedro, swinging lightly over the rail, disappeared foot by foot from view. "Farewell, old baboon! Farewell, heart of my heart!" he laughed joyously. "At Obydos I shall have you crowned——"

"King of the Monkeys," interrupted Harry with his heavy guffaw. "And at Obydos I'll have you tarred and feathered—tarred and feathered, you Dago, if you know what that means."

Pedro's two companions, obviously mechanics, pushed off. The motor-boat began moving gently and almost noiselessly away. But after it had gone a certain distance the crepitation of its powerful engines broke out, shattering with an effect of astonishing audacity the sullen stillness of the night.

Harry, who had been staring after the boat, turned abruptly and went to the wheel-house. "Half speed again," said he to Joao. Then, meditatively, he approached the wire-gauze cage.

After a moment a quiet voice came from inside. "You'll have a few explanations to give to-morrow, won't you?"

"Just what I was thinking," returned Harry.

Stella's laugh, discreetly low, sounded through the gauze. "*Viva la revoluçao.* Please enroll me. I'm on your side."

"Are you?" said Harry quite eagerly.

"Rather!" said Stella.

"Good girl!" said Harry. And as there was no answer to this, he moved away and presently went down to bed.

Stella was so excited that she couldn't sleep; and perhaps that was as well, for two hours later a cold dew began to fall, and in a short time the thermometer had dropped about twenty degrees. Shivering, she retreated to her cabin and there, under blankets, dozed until nine o'clock.

Chapter 12

WHEN she looked out of the porthole the *Clio* was tearing along at a great pace through a ruffled, yellow flood which was quite unlike the black, glassy water of the previous day. The southern shore was a long way off, and when she came on deck and searched the northern horizon there was no sign of land to be discovered. A low dull sky linked itself in the misty distance to the turbid stream. This was the real Amazon at last! The scene was grey; the air felt clammy and cold.

There was no one on deck; and when she looked into the saloon—no one. Curiosity drove her in search of company. She felt sure that the occurrence of the previous night must have given rise to gossip; and gossip would soon carry the news of Harry's talk with the handsome young stranger all over the ship. Whose cabin should she visit? She was not on terms of real intimacy with any of the women on board. Intimacies with women were not in her line. By a process of elimination she fixed upon Olga.

Olga was at her dressing-table, manicuring herself. She looked rather cross.

"Didn't you hear something like a motor-boat last night?" Stella inquired.

Olga said yes. It had wakened her up.

"I wonder who it was," said Stella.

Olga didn't know and obviously didn't care. "I think I shall go and see Dr. McLaren," she went on. "I'm feeling quite ill. And I'm sure it's from one of those awful dishes Harry gave us for dinner."

Stella murmured sympathy.

"Macpherson—my maid—says that everybody's out of sorts to-day," Olga continued. "As for the poor captain, he's worse. It's the sudden change of temperature. Don't you call it disgustingly cold?"

Olga's manner was friendly enough in spite of her crossness. She had begun to see that Stella was not the abandoned creature she had taken her for at first. This unfavourable judgment had been brought about by an accident which, early in the cruise, had apprised her of Stella's relations with Hugo. This discovery had greatly shocked her, but now she was getting over it. Indeed she considered that in comparison with Angela, Stella was a very dove. What Stella *did* mattered less than what Angela *was*.

Of all the guests on board the *Clio* Olga was at heart the least self-confident, the least self-satisfied, the most self-critical. Not only was she morbidly sensitive to public opinion, but she had an exaggerated sense of *noblesse oblige*. She set herself impossibly high standards not only of acting but of thinking and feeling. Had she been a young man and failed to get killed in the War she would have died of shame. Her showy manner was intended to conceal her natural shyness; and her affected ease produced a sense of strain because she was in effect always straining after a quality that eluded her.

Although her family was aristocratic, no member of it had ever belonged to the "smart set." That they could boast of an unusual number of distinguished men was, in her eyes, small compensation for the lack of that particular gift which they did not possess. They weren't able to cut a dash. That was it. They didn't carry a *panache* with style. So here Olga, notwithstanding her high principles, high courage, and high code of honour, came round to much the same position as the despised and disliked Angela. Moreover she respected principles, courage, and honour primarily because they were good form.

Dimly Olga was conscious that she and Angela had certain traits in common. Angela liked to keep her aware of it by a slightly impudent familiarity. Her smile often said: "We understand each other well enough, my dear. But whilst I am completely indifferent to *your* opinion of *me*, you simply hate *my* seeing through *you*."

What Olga was beginning to appreciate in Stella was her satisfactory unlikeness to Angela. On this particular morning she was feeling better disposed towards her than ever before. The reason was that she suspected Hugo of getting tired of his mistress. And her amour-propre demanded that she should soon get a husband.

The two young women had not been together many minutes before there came a knock at the door, and Angela, followed by Francis, pressed into the room. Francis's face wore an expression of importance and concern.

"Have you heard the latest?" he inquired.

"No."

"Well, here it is! Yellow fever has broken out at Para."

"Nonsense!" said Stella after a brief pause.

"Nonsense!" echoed Francis angrily. "My dear girl, I *know* it. The people there are dying like flies. They say it's going to be worse than the last outbreak, when three-quarters of the population died, and the rest deserted the town."

Francis's accents were sufficiently convincing to produce another silence, at the end of which Angela giggled.

"Give me a cigarette, Francis," she begged.

"Good God! What rot you talk!" exclaimed Stella robustly.

Olga looked at Stella. "How do you know it's rot?" she inquired.

"Oh! Because Francis says it," returned Stella.

Angela laughed with a sweetness that goaded Francis to exasperation.

"You needn't believe me if you don't want to, but the facts are these. An official from Para overhauled us last night in a fast motor-boat, he boarded the ship, and Harry was called up out of his cabin. The two talked together for about half an hour during which Joao, who was in the wheel-house——"

"Damned lies!" growled Harry, stepping into the open doorway.

Francis looked abashed, but not for more than a second. "Well! I'm delighted to hear it," he returned with a laugh and a shrug. "But, with all due respect, I fancied I heard a motor-boat."

"There *was* a motor-boat, Harry," said Olga.

Harry sighed and closed his eyes. His mother's voice could be heard calling him from the end of the passage.

"All right, mother dear," he returned in a tone of humorous weariness. "Your little Harry is coming."

After he had gone, Francis turned to the others with an expressive gesture.

"A perfect pet, isn't he? But," and his voice grew mysterious again, "if it isn't yellow fever, *what* is it?"

As Harry came into her cabin Lady Oswestry looked up at him meditatively from her arm-chair. Her toilet was finished; but she was still in her wrapper. Harry greeted her with a kiss.

"How well you look this morning!" And he lowered himself majestically into a chair opposite.

"What are all these rumours?" asked his mother with a touch of fretfulness. "In heaven's name, what are you up to now, my darling?"

Harry waved a hand, and smiled reassuringly.

As a matter of fact Lady Oswestry was not greatly disturbed. The doctor had, indeed, told her that he rather suspected Harry of dabbling in revolutionary politics. But she didn't think the doctor *could* be right. She had been trying to interest her eldest son in home politics for the last ten years and had failed completely. She couldn't conceive that Harry really meant anything. So all she said was: "Harry, darling, I don't want to be tiresome, but you *must* think of all the young people on board. You *must* remember your responsibility."

"That I promise!" returned Harry. His tone was grave, decisive. It seemed to satisfy her; at any rate, after a moment she picked up a hand-mirror and began studying herself.

"Mosquitoes been getting at you?" inquired Harry with concern.

She pointed dismally to a spot upon her cheek.

"Humph! Well, they've got at Angela too," said Harry.

There was a silence. Then he observed: "Hugo and Stella are cooling off, don't you think?"

His mother frowned. "I hope so."

Harry, lying back with eyes shut, smiled. "Angela was up to mischief last night."

Lady Oswestry paused before making any reply. Harry was touching the outskirts of the subject which held the first place in her mind. She had been watching Sir James very closely during the last two or three days, and she was no longer sure whether she would—or could—marry him. Her son's words filled her with an intense curiosity to learn whether he was favourable to the alliance or not. But she was shy of asking him.

"Thank heaven, Hugo doesn't show any signs of weakness in that direction." She said this in order to draw Harry out. Sir James's dalliance with Angela had not escaped her. But had Harry observed more than she?

"Awful responsibility for you—these unmarried young women on board," remarked Harry smilingly.

His mother laughed. "All the men are of an age to look after themselves, except perhaps Hugo. However," she added, "I'm not sure that the young men aren't wiser than the old ones."

Harry, echoing her laugh, looked straight into her eyes. "Whatever happens, this cruise was a good notion of yours." He pronounced this firmly, then got up and gave her another kiss.

Lady Oswestry felt that she had received her answer. He would approve, whatever her decision might be.

She smiled up at him with tenderness. "My darling, promise me again that you are not doing anything foolish. You won't get us all into difficulties just for the sake of a joke?"

Harry patted her on the shoulder. "Don't worry. This little shipload of youth and beauty shan't suffer. But as to doing nothing foolish,—damn it! you must tell me first what's folly and what isn't. *I* don't know."

His mother gave a deep sigh. This had always been Harry's attitude, and it baffled her.

"You must be serious," she said rather weakly.

"Seems to me the serious people are often the most foolish," replied Harry. "Well! I must go and see the poor old skipper. There's a serious man for you. And so is Mr. Wilkinson; but, deary me . . . !" And he lounged heavily out of the room.

A little later, when Lady Oswestry came on deck, the sun was shining and the scene looked more cheerful. Then someone pointed out that the water ahead was becoming olive green all along the southern bank. Yes, explained the professor, that was because they were nearing the confluence with the Tapajos, whose clear waters flowed side by side with those of the Amazon for several miles before being lost in the opaque flood.

Shortly after this Santarem came into view. It had been understood that the *Clio* would put in there.

The professor had described a delicious beach of white sand, up the Tapajos, about a mile beyond Santarem, where one could bathe in safety. There was consequently an outcry of expostulation when, after hovering about off the little town for a quarter of an hour, the *Clio* suddenly sheered aside and resumed her journey up-stream.

Lady Oswestry shrugged. " You must ask Harry about it," she said. " *I'm* not responsible, my children."

Harry was in the wheel-house talking to Joao in Portuguese. Joao looked puzzled and sulky.

" We're going to Obydos," said Harry. " Much better place Obydos. If we push on now we shall get there to-night."

" But the bathing ! " cried Olga and Mary. " Who wants to bathe at Obydos in the horrid yellow Amazon water ! "

Harry was silent for a minute, then he said :

" Well ! If you want to know the truth, it's at Santarem that yellow fever has just broken out. I wouldn't take you there for a million."

There were murmurs of incredulity at this. The professor, when appealed to, rolled his eyes, wiped his glasses and opened his mouth ; but refused to say anything.

During the hour of siesta the *Clio* pushed on at top speed, the throb of her engines being unusually noticeable as she fought against the current. At tea everyone was in a better humour ; the weather was agreeably warm again, and the effects of Harry's birthday dinner seemed to be passing off.

" I spent several months at Santarem last year,"

said the professor. "It's a pleasant little place of about four thousand inhabitants."

"Harry," cried Mary, "you promise, don't you, that we shall stop at Obydos? What is Obydos like, professor?"

The answer was non-committal. "I don't know it so well. It is a great centre for cacao. It is also a garrison town. At one time it was fortified. It commands the Amazon at a point where the river is only one mile across."

The *Clio* was making such good way that there was every chance of reaching Obydos before nightfall. Two or three times during the course of the day Joao had taken her across the wide river from the right bank to the left or *vice versa*, his object being to avoid shoals, to dodge inconvenient islands, or to escape the full strength of the current. At sundown, when Obydos was not more than five miles off, the *Clio* was steaming along the northern shore quite close to the forest which spread some yards over the water. The trees here, supporting themselves on a scaffold of pallid roots, served in turn as a support to a great variety of vines which hung in festoons from branch to branch, knitting the whole green mass together in an intricate serpentine tangle. Harry was in the wheel-house talking to Joao while Joachim stood at the wheel. Harry's field-glasses were up to his eyes most of the time; he seemed watchful and kept asking how soon Obydos would come into view.

For his part old Joao was sulky. He had recently told his son that he was beginning to think the Commandante was not quite right in the head. And

this impression of his was destined to receive an
early and vigorous confirmation. For, all at once,
Harry broke into vehement imprecations and, as
Joao afterwards expressed it, assumed the countenance
of a fiend. At the same instant, too, he rushed to
the wheel, hurling Joachim aside, and whirled the
spokes round in such a manner that the unfortunate
Clio slewed violently to starboard and ran her nose
deep into the jungle before anyone had time to do
anything but gasp or yell.

For a few moments, until she came to a standstill,
there was indeed a dreadful medley of sounds.
Joachim and Joao were howling in Portuguese, the
ship's officers were shouting warnings and commands,
branches were tearing and cracking on every side,
and the women servants below were lustily giving
tongue.

Joao was apoplectic. "Insensate bastard, fruit of
the dunghill, and offspring of hell!" he shouted into
Harry's face. 'Behold what calamity! Now we
shall all perish! And it is your work!"

"Steady, old boy!" returned Harry, patting him
on the back. "Steady and calm! Merry and bright!
Every cloud has a silver lining. Moreover, I pray you,
if your eyes are not too bloodshot, take a look at
those two little black things bobbing along in the
water."

So saying he gripped Joao's arm and pointed.
But Joao did not yet understand.

"Have a look through these," said Harry, unslinging
his field-glasses.

Joao looked.

"Well!" said Harry.

After a moment Joao's face took on an awestruck expression. He put down the glasses and gazed at Harry questioningly.

"Mines?" he whispered.

"Can't be anything else."

"But how? But why?"

Harry shrugged. "Revolution, I fancy."

"Holy Mother of God!"

"May the blessed saints intercede for my soul!" ejaculated Joachim, tugging at a chain round his neck from which was suspended a small metal image of his patron saint.

"Revolution!" murmured Joao more calmly. And with a kind of complacency he added: "Well! It was time."

Harry shook him by the hand. "I can see," he declared warmly, "that you, like me, are the friend of justice and liberty."

Chapter 13

MEANWHILE the hubbub on deck was far from having died down. The engineer had reversed the engines, but the only result was to make the *Clio* shiver from stem to stern and to bring down foliage and dead branches in a rain upon the deck. Nor was this all that fell; a large assortment of Brazilian fauna descended; notably two fat iguanas measuring about four feet from nose to tail, a great number and variety of smaller lizards, several nestsful of fledglings, a long thin tree snake, a host of tree frogs, some remarkable caterpillars about as thick as a man's thumb, and a prodigious quantity of other insects, including a whole wasp's nest which broke into fragments at Francis's feet. It was therefore not surprising that Francis's voice dominated all the other human outcries. In fact Francis continued to roar like a young bull whilst he precipitated himself down the companion-way, made for the nearest bathroom, and got under the shower bath which he turned on at full strength.

By good fortune there was no casualty more serious than this. The heavier of the boughs with which the deck was strewn had touched no one. But the poor *Clio* herself was sadly scratched and torn. Her aerials were nowhere to be seen; parts of the rigging hung in tatters; the " meat safe " was a crumpled heap; and a great deal of broken window glass lay about the deck.

When Harry emerged from the wheel-house and acknowledged that the deed was his, hard looks were levelled at him. But he explained. And while he was explaining a terrific detonation took place; about five hundred yards astern a thick column of Amazon water rose up into the air; and in the ensuing silence fragments of splintered log fell back, splash, splash, into the yellow foam. "There, but for the grace of God, goes the poor old *Clio*," commented Harry. And after that no further criticism of his action was heard.

A little later, after he had hurried off to consult with the first officer and the engineer, Lady Oswestry, looking thoughtful, betook herself to her cabin. The doctor, she was told, was attending to Mr. Tilling's wasp stings. She sent him a message to come to her as soon as he could.

Whilst waiting, she meditated upon Harry's character, not angrily, but with resignation.

When the doctor appeared they stood looking at one another for a moment. The doctor's eyes were twinkling; at last she could not but smile.

"Oh! I've not forgotten that you warned me about Harry. But all the same——"

Her sentence was cut short. A heavy wave of sound shook the air. It was the booming of artillery.

"Really!" And she now spoke in a voice of outrage. "This is beyond a joke!"

The doctor agreed; but traces of his amusement lingered. If his voice was grave the lines round his mouth betrayed him.

"It's obviously a revolution," said Lady Oswestry.

"I'm afraid——" began the doctor.

"And Harry is in it."

"Well——" said the doctor.

"What more do you know?" she inquired.

"Nothing."

She sat down and considered.

"I can't help thinking that Harry is behaving very badly. He promised me only this morning that he would be sensible."

Harry put his head in at the door.

"It's all right. The propellers are clear and we are not badly stuck."

"Harry, come in, please," said his mother. "I want to talk to you."

Harry came in.

Lady Oswestry put her hand up to her forehead. A sudden light had flashed upon her.

"Tell me!" she said. "Who was that little man you saw in New York?"

Harry looked vague. "What little man?"

"Oh, come, Harry!" said the doctor persuasively. "I know you saw Andrade in New York, and once or twice since then it has shot across my mind——"

"Andrade!" exclaimed Lady Oswestry. "Yes! That's the man I mean."

Harry was walking up and down frowning at the carpet.

"We haven't time to go into all that now," he said at last. "We've got to get things ship-shape for the night." He paused. "In a word the situation is this: The revolution has broken out. Para is in the hands of the revolutionaries. So is Obydos, unless there has been some fiasco there. And I have no doubt that Manaos by this time is in their hands as well. In fact you can take it as certain that the whole of Amazonia has thrown off its allegiance to Brazil." He laughed. " One of the beauties of the situation is that a portion of the Federal Government's fleet, which was paying a visit to Para, has declared for the new Amazonian State. In Para, it seems, hardly a shot was fired."

" You learnt all this from your visitor last night ? "

" Yes. That's Andrade's younger brother. I met him for the first time in Para the other day. That boy is a jewel—straight as they make 'em. Those two brothers are running this little show."

" And you are mixed up in it ! " observed Lady Oswestry bitterly.

" Oh, no ! " returned Harry with a careless gesture. " Not really."

There was a silence.

" Well, my dear Harry, the sooner we clear out the better," said the doctor. " You agree to that, I hope ? "

Harry nodded. " I do."

" Why did you bring us up here ? " demanded Lady Oswestry with some indignation. " After last night you might at least have turned back."

" I had to see how things were going up-river," returned Harry, speaking slowly and thoughtfully. " I didn't dare put into Santarem ; that little town may still be in the hands of the other party. But I *must* get into touch with Para and Manaos by cable— from Obydos. I must go on to Obydos to-night. . . ."

"How do you propose to go?" asked the doctor. "By boat?"

"I'm thinking that over," replied Harry evasively. "Perhaps I shall go by land. It can't be more than a couple of miles or so."

Lady Oswestry threw up her hands. "Dear doctor," she said, almost tearfully, "do try to make him take you into his confidence. Perhaps he will be more open with you than with me."

As she was speaking, repeated knocks at her door made it plain that Harry's presence was urgently demanded elsewhere.

"I'll be back in one second," said Harry, making his escape.

In the meantime Hugo and Sir James had, as Mr. Simpson expressed it, "been keeping the ladies quiet." As a matter of fact, however, none of the ladies had exhibited any emotion other than a pleased and excited interest in the occurrences of the last hour. Their principal occupation for the time being was to keep clear of the menagerie which had invaded the ship. For it was not only on deck that animals swarmed; they had come in through the portholes on the starboard side; and, as many of the ports were jammed and could not be closed, they continued to crawl, flutter, or hop in with the utmost eagerness. Angela's quarters had suffered the most. A great branch had thrust itself through the portholes and stretched right across her cabin, which it rendered temporarily uninhabitable.

All the forward cabins, moreover, were pervaded by a strange musky smell. The professor sniffed and declared it was the usual smell of mangrove swamps.

"I advise you all," he said, "to be particularly careful with your mosquito nets to-night. We haven't been troubled by insects so far, but here we are likely to be besieged."

Joachim, when he had recovered from his first agitation, was full of even graver warnings. The musky smell, *he* said, came from a crocodile's lair in a hole under the bank. The trees surrounding the *Clio* were of a kind that gave off a poisonous gas during the hours of darkness. Pointing up into the dark foliage overhead, he discerned, he said, bunches of vampire bats waiting to suck human blood. And it was well known that boa-constrictors thirty feet long boarded steam-yachts whenever they got a chance.

Dinner, that evening, was a very animated meal. The conversation turned upon two subjects—the animals on board, and the revolution. One of the iguanas had been seized by the tail and slung overboard, but the other had scuttled down the companion-way and was presumably hiding in one of the cabins. The chatter was tremendous. Francis's face had swollen into a pink pudding and it hurt him to open his mouth; but he talked incessantly all the same.

Upon the revolution Mr. Wilkinson provided some interesting historical commentaries. "In 1892 the State of Rio Grande do Sul revolted; in 1909 there was a naval insurrection; not many months ago, as you remember, the Sao Paulo revolt took place; and since then there has been another small insurrection in the Federal fleet. All those risings were crushed, and I don't suppose this one has a much better chance."

"Can't agree with you there," replied Harry. "Geographically and economically, the upper half of Brazil has precious little connection with the lower half. Between Para and Rio de Janeiro no communication is possible by land, and the sea route is about three thousand miles. What can the Federal Government do? They can't send their fleet to Para. It would get blown up by mines before it had gone more than a mile or two down the estuary. To land troops on that coast is utterly impracticable. They might try a blockade, but that would be difficult and expensive; besides, it would be months, if not years, before the Paraense suffered any serious inconvenience."

Hugo observed that Stella was listening to this with sparkling eyes, and he felt some annoyance. The coldness between them had been increasing apace. He didn't like the way Stella hung upon Harry's words. It was true, everyone at the table seemed to be more or less in favour of the revolution—even Mr. Wilkinson was separatist in his sympathies,—but Stella exhibited an altogether extravagant partisanship.

Animated by a spirit of opposition Hugo took the other side. "I know nothing of Brazilian politics, but I doubt whether Amazonia has anything to gain by separating itself from the richer and more industrious half of Brazil. Left to itself, the——"

Stella interrupted him. "Left to itself Amazonia would be twenty times as well off as it is now. Since 1852 it has turned into the Federal Treasury more than one million contos of reis of which barely 250,000 contos have been spent in the district, and that chiefly as the cost of collection."

Having spoken, she blushed slightly under Hugo's satirical gaze. "How well-informed you are!" he murmured.

"Stella is quite right," said Harry. "I can assure you that Amazonia has been steadily and systematically sucked dry by the Federal Government for the last fifty or sixty years; so far from having received help, it has been handicapped by a fiscal policy which has made development almost impossible. The taxes upon imports, to take a flagrant injustice, are such as to make the price of foreign goods almost prohibitive. The State of Para pays more to Rio in taxes than the total amount of its own budget. No wonder the finances of Amazonia are in a bad way! To put things straight a cessation of the exorbitant payments to Rio would suffice."

As she listened to Harry, Lady Oswestry's face clouded. She said:

"For years I've tried to interest you in English politics. And now you are taking a far greater interest in the politics of Brazil!"

To this Harry made no reply.

Out on deck, after dinner, the silence and immobility of the ship felt very strange. The forward half of her was thickly wedged in among trees whose snaky roots rose as much as ten feet above the present water level. In the manner of their growth, the professor said, these trees closely resembled the mangrove of West Africa. On the starboard side the forest kept touch with the *Clio* right up to the stern. The whole of the deck was overhung by foliage; a magnificent tree, not unlike an acacia, leaned over her amidships with a protective air;

its friendly branches almost dipping into the water
on the other side. At a distance of about twenty
feet from the *Clio's* bows the river bank lifted itself
out of the shallow water, presenting a slope of brown
mud. But even by day this was not easily discernible
through the intervening tangle.

The *Clio* was no longer a free and mobile portion
of the civilisation to which she belonged. One felt
that she had become a part of the forest, a permanent
feature in the surrounding scene.

The doctor and Hugo leaned over the side, staring
at the river faintly silvered by a young moon.

" It would be tiresome if we were to find ourselves
badly stuck here," said the doctor slowly.

The idea that they might after all be "badly
stuck" had passed through the minds of more than
one person on board. The roots and lianas surrounding
the ship had a tentacular aspect; they looked as
if they had caught the poor *Clio* in their grip. Hugo
made no reply. He was feeling depressed, besides
being not a little angry with Harry, who, if he had
saved them from being blown up, was none the less
responsible for their present predicament.

A few paces off Lady Oswestry, Harry, and the
professor were conferring together.

" I'm not going to let you go to Obydos alone,"
said Harry's mother, fixing him with determination.

" If you are thinking of walking there," began the
professor.

" You want to walk! by night! through the
jungle!" exclaimed Lady Oswestry, raising her
voice in horror.

" My dear lady," interposed the professor, " please

let me reassure you. What lies between us and
Obydos is not jungle, but a big cacao plantation.
If your son prefers to walk I might be useful as a
guide."

"I want to make an unobtrusive entry into the
town," Harry confided a little later to the professor.
"You see there is a Federal garrison at Obydos—
about two hundred strong. It is pretty certain that
they have joined the revolutionaries, but Pedro
may have been over-sanguine about that."

"Would they be likely to know that you were a
partisan?" inquired the professor.

"They might. I can't be certain that spies in
Para did not track me down to the low pub where
Pedro and I used to meet."

Eventually the professor was accepted as guide.
By a gangway of planks roughly laid over and in
between the roots Harry and he made their way
ashore. For a minute or so the light from their
electric torches shone out among the trees, then all
became dark again except for the zigzagging spark
of an occasional fire-fly.

After they had disappeared the women retired
into the saloon, where they were safe from the
mosquitoes; whilst Hugo and Sir James continued
to pace the deck. Never had the latter felt fonder
of Hugo than now. The slightly complacent air
with which the young man protected his inward
sensitiveness had been dispelled by his present
griefs. Before Sir James, in particular, he felt no
need to dissimulate. At this moment he wore the
troubled face of a child.

Sir James began talking about Harry. "He ought

to have gone into politics. He has much more
talent in that direction than you. He reminds me
of Disraeli. He has the cunning, the practical
imagination and the histrionic sense of the Jew.
You, on the other hand, are really a doctrinaire, my
dear Hugo. Your politics rest upon first principles
which are fixed in your mind. You would have had
no chance of a hearing before the war. Now for the
second time in the world's history first principles are
being considered in politics. Personally, I believe
that the Liberal and Democratic principles of to-day
are as childish as those which inspired the French
Revolution. But they are doing mankind a great
service by arousing an intellectual opposition. In
the old days intellect and imagination were on the
side of the reformer. To-day sentimentality and
envy are the chief forces behind democracy, while the
brains and the imagination are with us. Until quite
recently the Conservative has relied largely upon
birth, wealth and influence. Among the Conservatives of to-day is the intellectual with a philosophy
and the enthusiast with a cause."

Sir James discoursed in this fashion because Hugo,
he knew, was not feeling talkative. And on his
side he did not wish to seem to be waiting for
confidences.

"It is perfectly obvious," he went on, "that Stella
and Mr. Wilkinson are sentimentalists. Mr. Wilkinson
belongs to the old ethical-sentimental school; Stella
is a rank practical revolutionary, but not one whit
less sentimental than Mr. Wilkinson in spite of her
contempt for Christian ethics. Harry is your true
politician and leader of men. The flaws in his

character are impatience and a passion for burlesque. He slides from the dignified comedy of a Disraeli into sheer clowning. What he's going to do with us all up here, God only knows!" And Sir James mingled a laugh and a sigh.

Hugo was saved from the necessity of making any reply by the appearance of the doctor. The latter informed them that the captain was better, but that one of the stewards had developed blood-poisoning from the bite of some insect. His case was pretty serious.

"I shall be surprised," said Sir James, after the doctor had hurried off, "I shall be more than surprised if we don't have a death on board before we get back to England. It's a presentiment."

"You'd better smoke," he went on, offering Hugo a cigarette, "the mosquitoes are getting lively. Yes, in the tropics death is always near, and the presentiment of death almost always justified. That is one of the charms of the tropics; you live on pleasant neighbourly terms with death; you are prevented from worrying about trifles and taking life too seriously. Death is seen as natural and familiar here. Personally, I should much prefer dying under a mangrove tree to dying in a London nursing home."

Chapter 14

THE evening passed restlessly. There was no knowing how long Harry would be, but no one could decide to retire. Bridge (of a desultory and conversational order) went on until after one o'clock when a distant sound of singing and cheering brought everyone running out on to the deck. A few minutes later lights appeared upon the water; several boats were rounding the bend that hid Obydos from view. Great was the excitement which broke out on board the *Clio*, and it was pleasantly coloured by the fact that the approaching crowd was unmistakably in the best of humours.

Before very long half a dozen large *montarias* or canoes came up, the foremost containing Harry and the professor. Two Brazilian officers in uniform accompanied them; the other *montarias* were filled with Brazilian gentry. Torches and lanterns amply illuminated the scene, to which a barbaric air was given by the native craft and bronze-backed native paddlers.

Harry's canoe was brought up to the companion-ladder and the two stepped out. Harry flourished his hat; cheers were raised; Harry made a brief speech in Portuguese; more cheers followed, and an outbreak of patriotic song. Then, after much waving of hands and an exchange of friendly banter, the *montarias* withdrew into the night.

When Harry stepped up on to the deck he was

looking well pleased. "Really it couldn't have passed off better," said he. "Splendid reception! Eh, professor?"

The professor nodded. A slight film of bewilderment lay over the habitual placidity of his features. Amid a general hubbub Harry and he were dragged into the saloon, and entreated to give a detailed account of their adventures.

" 'Pon my word," said Harry after helping himself to a large whisky and soda, " there's not much to tell. All went off according to plan. We toddled through the cacao plantation, tripping over an occasional anaconda, until we came to the outskirts of the town. Then, just as the Professor was saying that he must take his bearings, he fell over a donkey and broke his torch. However, he had had time to recognise the donkey as belonging to a friend of his, Jose Maria de san Christobel; and the donkey guided us to a small shack inside which, sure enough, we heard Jose Maria and his wife snoring like traction engines. It seemed a pity to disturb them so we wandered on through pitch darkness without ever meeting a soul until we came to a little terrace overlooking the river. There a political meeting was in progress. By ruffling my hair and assuming the expression of a Brazilian I passed unnoticed among the throng. Listening to the orator I discovered in a few seconds that all was well. The garrison has joined us, and the good citizens of Obydos are separatists to a man!"

Cheers greeted this piece of information. Harry took another pull at his whisky and soda, cast a lordly look around him and resumed:

"It was not long before the professor and I had embraced everyone within sight, mounted on to the platform and started making speeches. I told them——"

"Never mind what *you* told *them*, Harry dear," put in his mother; "let us know what they told you. As our lot seems to be cast in with the revolutionaries I do hope Para remains in their hands?"

"It does," returned Harry. "And what is more everything has gone in our favour at Manaos. I don't mind confessing to you now that I have been a little nervous about Manaos, because several warships of the Federal Fleet are up there, and if they had turned nasty they could have steamed down the river making things hot for everybody on the way. However, the Federal Fleet can generally be relied upon to rebel; and sure enough they all joined us except one wretched river monitor, the crew of which had recently got their pay and didn't realise that the Federal Government had paid them by mistake. So they *did* steam off,—and that, by the way, accounts for those mines. Yesterday morning the commander-in-chief at Obydos mistook a crocodile or something for that monitor and ordered the mines to be launched. Luckily there were only half a dozen which had been stolen off a warship last year by someone who thought they would come in useful on Guy Fawkes day. So that's that. We needn't worry about mines any more."

"How nice!" murmured Lady Oswestry, faintly sarcastic.

"Moreover," continued Harry, casting her a look

of dignified reproach, " owing to my being *persona grata* with the *de facto* government, tugs will be sent here to-morrow morning to drag us out of this little shrubbery, and I hope that by the evening we shall be steaming back to Para."

" But do we need assistance to get free ? " inquired his mother, opening her eyes.

" It might expedite matters," returned Harry evasively, and he added, " I have given them an incentive by undertaking to deliver some important despatches at Para."

" What about that little monitor ? " asked Francis.

" Yes," added Sir James, " what if it overtakes us and searches us and finds revolutionary despatches on board ? "

" I should eat the despatches piecemeal before anyone reached the ship," replied Harry firmly. " As you ought to know, James, that is *de rigeur* among men of honour.

There was a meditative silence.

" Look here, everybody ! " exclaimed Harry with a grin. " I guarantee that so long as I have any control over this little revolution it shall not rise above the level of ordinary musical comedy. There ! is that good enough for you ? "

" What about the mines and the firing ? " asked Francis.

" Damn it ! there must be a little firing," returned Harry. " That's an essential feature of all revolutions. But no one need get hurt."

" Did no one get hurt at Manaos ? " asked the professor mildly. " I thought I heard them saying the streets ran with blood."

"The streets at Manaos are rather apt to run with blood; and no one can regret it more than I." Harry sighed. "But if the wireless account is to be trusted, what happened there last night is nothing to what took place in 1910, when the State troops and the Federal troops and the Federal flotilla all began fighting together about nothing at all. If only I could have been at Manaos last night there probably wouldn't have been *any* bloodshed."

A smile went round.

"I mean it, gentlemen!" said Harry earnestly. "There is a large and excellent brewery in the centre of the town, and our troops made the mistake of attempting to defend it. *I* should have let the enemy capture it at once, and my tactics would have been sound. Because, as a matter of fact, half an hour after the opposing troops *had* entered the place they ceased to give us any further trouble."

There was a general laugh, in which Lady Oswestry joined, but with a note of vexation.

"Dearest mother," continued Harry, "surely it is obvious that from your point of view the line which I have chosen could not be bettered. Our chances of getting away quick are vastly enhanced by my being on such good terms with the new government. To begin with, Joao and Joachim would desert us at once if they weren't certain of my sympathies. Do you know where they are at this moment?"

Lady Oswestry shook her head.

"In Obydos, drinking to the success of the revolution. But they have promised me to come back to-morrow morning, and they will. They would get into trouble with the authorities if they didn't."

Again there was a meditative silence, whilst Harry let his words sink in.

"Similarly, with regard to the *Clio's* position here. To tell you the honest truth, Veeder now thinks we should find it difficult to get clear unaided. Our bows are pretty deeply wedged in mud, the river is falling, and we can't use our screw without risk on account of the infernal mangrove roots. We depend upon getting someone to haul us out."

Lady Oswestry shrugged. To recriminate or argue with Harry appeared, as usual, unprofitable. Besides, it was getting very late. She rose, and the women all retired; nor were the men long in following their example.

To sleep, however, was not easy. There was no draught on the stationary ship; no breath of air found its way into her sheltered bower. The humid atmosphere was laden with smells from the mud and the surrounding vegetation. Moreover here the travellers for the first time became acutely aware of the life of the forest. The intense stillness was broken by furtive rustlings, sudden scuffling noises, the occasional snap of a dry twig, or a sudden splash in the water. Sometimes a frog would give an unexpected croak or a bird emit a startled cry. And these sounds were so close that one felt oneself plunged into an exciting intimacy with the natural life of which they spoke. The *Clio* had been taken as an unwilling neophyte into the penetralia of the God of Amazonia.

As the hours wore on, the stillness, the dampness

and the heat became suffocating. Then at last
patter, patter, patter came the rain upon the foliage;
and a few instants later it was a downpour. The
leafy roof, soon saturated, let the water down in
noisy streamlets upon the deck. "Well, it can't go
on like this for long," thought the sleepless ones,
"and the rain will make the air cooler." But they
were mistaken. It did go on, and the expected
coolness never came.

In the morning it was still raining; the forest
steamed up into the rain; wisps of vapour curled
over the river. No one went out of doors excepting
Harry, who hurried off to Obydos in a motor-boat.

"What is the betting that the tugs really *will*
appear to-day?" And Sir James looked round the
smoking-room with a smile of patient cynicism.
"From my knowledge of South American ways,
I should say that we shall be lucky if we get any help
within the next three weeks."

No one made any reply to this except Hugo, who
emitted a low groan.

Sir James drew his chair close up to the professor's
and leaned towards him confidentially.

"Tell me!" said he: "What is your private view
of the situation? Dear Harry's accounts are quite
amusing. . . . But I should very much like to hear
what *you* have to say."

The professor pulled his beard. "Everything
Lord Oswestry told you was substantially accurate,"
he returned after a pause. But his tone and his gaze
were, Sir James thought, altogether too deliberative.

"What I can't understand," the latter went on,
"is how Harry, a foreigner and a stranger in the

land, has succeeded—as he apparently has—in imposing himself——"

"It's most remarkable," the professor agreed.

"Do the good people of Obydos really take him seriously?"

"Certainly. Young Andrade has prepared the way for him."

"But who exactly are these Andrades?" inquired Sir James in a tone of mystification. "I only know them as a London firm of Brazilian merchants. Are they very powerful out here?"

The professor looked at Sir James. "The Andrades," he replied impressively, "are virtually the supreme rulers over a tract of country about as large as the whole of France. Their kingdom is right up at the head-waters of the Amazon where Peru, Bolivia and Brazil meet. In the days of the rubber boom they amassed an immense fortune—and that in spite of the intolerable tribute exacted by the Federal Government—and without cruelty to the native population."

While Sir James was considering this, the doctor came up and was drawn into the conversation.

"Harry appears to have known the elder brother, Mario, for some years," he said. "And when we were in New York he happened to run across him again. There he learnt that a revolution was brewing, and thought no doubt that it would be amusing to join in. He has admitted to me that he practically promised Mario that he would go to Para and help Pedro with advice. Pedro's right-hand man, Marco Pinto, had just died of a sudden fever, so the young revolutionary stood in need of someone to help him,

someone of greater years and experience than himself.
Mario himself couldn't go because he would be required
in Europe to look after the financial and diplomatic
side of the affair after the *coup* had taken place."

They went on discussing Harry all the morning,
while the rain came steadily down. The professor
was mildly amused by the general indignation at the
change of weather. "This," he announced, "is
what you have to expect in Brazil. Hitherto we
have been quite unusually lucky."

A little comfort was taken in the thought that
perhaps the river would rise and facilitate the *Clio's*
extrication. But the hours meanwhile dragged
heavily enough. The travellers, accustomed to
constant movement, to a shifting scene, to a succession
of small distractions, were now made to realise that
the further you depart from civilisation the more
slowly does time flow. Its pace on the Amazon
seemed to be regulated for requirements that were
certainly sub-human. One could fancy it set for the
boa-constrictor which takes a leisurely fifteen minutes
to move from one position of repose to another.

During the whole of this day an unconscious effort
was made to keep up the tempo of London. Bridge
was played busily; letters were written busily;
gossip went on busily; and Sir James carried on a
busy dalliance with Angela. This he did, first,
because it amused him and, secondly, because he was
feeling slightly vexed with Lady Oswestry. She
had been letting him see all too clearly that her sons
occupied the first place in her heart. He perceived
that in marrying her he would be accepting a secondary
position—he would become the poor husband of a

rich woman whose ambition was fixed upon her sons.
Now Sir James was prepared to yield place to the
younger generation; but not so completely, not in so
marked a fashion, as this. His pride, his vanity,
rebelled. He felt tempted to give proof that he was
still able and ready to occupy the centre of the
stage.

During the hour of siesta, Angela who was sharing
Mary's cabin, startled her companion by coming
out with the question:

"Darling, if Sir James asks me to marry him,
what do you think I had better say?"

Then, as Mary sat up and stared at her, in the
same languid tone she went on: "In any case I
can see that I'm going to have a terribly awkward
time with poor dear Marion. Imagine, if we're
stuck here for weeks and weeks, and Marion glares
at me all the time as she has to-day!"

"She hasn't glared at you at all!" exclaimed Mary
with some heat.

"Oh, my dear!" And Angela smiled indulgently.
"But then you don't notice things."

Mary was silent. She found the topic embarrassing.
Her private thoughts were that it would be lovely if
Aunt Marion and Sir James married, and that Angela
was more of a cat than she had ever suspected.

Seeing that there was nothing to be got out of
her in the way of comment or reported gossip, Angela
began chattering about clothes. The subjects upon
which they met most easily were love, clothes, and
the way to live your life.

Mary, however, had never talked to Angela about
Gerald. She had an instinct not to depart from

generalities. The intimacy between the two girls, although very close, was severely circumscribed by Mary's fastidiousness and Angela's discretion; for Angela, who took pleasure in offending Olga's taste, had no wish to offend Mary's.

"Darling," she said presently, "I shall have to sleep here again to-night. My cabin, you know, is still in a frightful mess." She was reclining on Mary's divan and glancing through a heap of old letters as she spoke. After a minute Mary, who was watching her, gave a slight start; she had caught sight of Gerald's handwriting.

"Oh! What's that?" she unthinkingly exclaimed. "Isn't it——" And blushing, she broke off.

Angela raised her head and gave a faint, slow smile.

"A letter from Gerald Acton? Yes."

"You never told me you knew him," said Mary in confusion.

Angela laughed gently. "Why should I, darling? You've never breathed his name to me;—have you?"

Mary was silent.

"I've known him for a long time," continued Angela, looking at Mary with a kind of mocking affection. "I think he's awfully sweet."

"Do you?" Mary's tone was cold.

"I've just met him at dances," Angela explained, as she went on turning over her letters. "I don't really know him *well*."

All at once another letter of Gerald's came to light. Angela picked it up and glanced through it. Her expression betrayed a slight embarrassment. She said: "One mustn't show letters to other people,

must one ? But I don't want you to think this is
a love-letter. And, anyhow, it was written *years*
ago."

Mary summoned a careless laugh. "What *does*
it matter ? I really don't mind, darling ! It would
be strange if Gerald hadn't ever made love to you.
I have no illusions about him."

Angela smiled again, and somehow or other Mary
felt pretty sure that between Gerald and Angela
there was the *camaraderie* of gay sinners—nothing
more.

Later, however, when she was by herself, she
became thoughtful. It was odd, perhaps, but she
objected more to Gerald's being on terms of friendship with Angela than to his making love to her.
Angela was pretty enough to make any man desirous
of kissing her, but to be a friend of Angela's one had
to be unfastidious. Her own relations with Angela
were, she realised, peculiar. They depended absolutely upon Angela's being impersonal. That Angela
was equally impersonal with Gerald was not easily
to be believed. In other words, after putting all
questions of infidelity aside, there remained in
Gerald's character a streak that was distasteful to
her. And Mary felt that this particular streak
mattered deeply.

At sundown the rain ceased and she paced the
deck in company with Hugo, whose mood seemed
attuned to hers. He told her that Harry had just
returned from Obydos with the promise that assistance should be sent to the *Clio* the next day.

"And then, I suppose," said Mary dreamily, "we
shall turn straight back."

All of a sudden she felt sorry that they were going back. She was seized with the wish that she could be left behind. And when she said this to Hugo, after a moment's silence he surprised her by replying that he had been taken with a similar desire. He, too, would have liked to remain in the wilds, to camp out, and fish, and hunt, and live a primitive life, away from all society.

Chapter 15

THE next morning was bright and sunny. So it was arranged that while the work of freeing the *Clio* was being carried out the whole party should go for a walk in the forest. They set out with gaiety, their interest being stimulated by the thought that this would probably be their only opportunity of viewing scenery typical of a region as large as the whole of Western Europe. There was joking and laughter as they shuffled precariously along the rude gangway connecting the ship with the shore. The planks were excessively slippery, being already overgrown with a minute fungus. Hundreds of small crabs were scuttling about on the roots just above the ugly yellow-green water. Dew still dripped in heavy drops from the big dark leaves overhead. All glistening with wet, the roots and twisting branches of the trees had a particularly snake-like aspect.

From the planks one stepped on to a slope of softish mud from which there rose a faint steam. Here the mangroves gradually gave place to other trees. For about five hundred yards the ground rose gently and then one entered into the gloom of the cacao plantation. The professor explained that this particular plantation had been abandoned; the trees were old and had been allowed to interlace too thickly. Their black trunks and black low growing branches supported a roof of foliage which excluded nearly all light. The dead leaves underfoot formed a black paste. This region had its own peculiar smell, different from that of the riverside. The silence would have been absolute but for the harsh cries of parrots and macaws, flying about, invisible, above the leafy roof. There was no temptation to linger here. Everyone was glad when, half a mile farther on, the cacao-trees ended and the real forest began.

The colour of the forest was grey. Smooth, pale trunks went up, branchless, into a grey ambiguity. A mist of a pallid, starved foliage hung a hundred feet overhead. The world of sunlight and greenery lay somewhere above. From below it was completely out of sight. One had the sense of being very far beneath the surface of life.

The ground still rose gradually, and as it rose the trees grew larger and more widely spaced. They supported themselves with immense buttresses; lianas clasped them, hung from their limbs, and dangled hungry air-roots overhead. The soil underfoot was a spongy leaf-mould upon which grew pale fungi. In places there was moss; but not even the moss was strongly green.

The party had been warned not to stray. They followed the professor in a straggling line. He alone talked; Lady Oswestry and Mary, who were at his side, listened, or seemed to listen. The others followed silent.

It was not easy to be conversational in the forest. Francis held out longest. He lost his chattiness only when it became quite obvious that no one was paying any attention. After that he walked along silent, but with an air of determined jauntiness. Swinging a malacca cane, a long amber cigarette-holder gripped between his teeth, he had the air of considering whether he should pop into his tailor's or visit his manicurist.

Behind him came Stella and Olga, both quite subdued; their rare comments were exchanged in an undertone.

Sir James, Mr. Wilkinson and Hugo brought up the rear. They stared and said nothing.

Sir James was glad that Angela had not come. The forest was so terribly old and grey; it reminded him that he himself was getting old and grey. In Bond Street his age did not matter; here it mattered. Had he been a native it would have been his part to sit all day in unconsidered idleness watching the young braves equip themselves for the hunt.

All the life of this world was up above in the green surface spreading out under the sun; the twilight region below was the lumber-room for things outworn —withered leaves, empty husks, perished branches. It was the abode of silence—no sun here, no wind, no rain—no life! And yet, yes, life! These trunks were the pillars of the present, dark yet living conduits for the sap which ran to feed the green juicy leaves and coloured flowers unfolding in skiey freedom above.

Over the whole party there brooded a heavy pensiveness. The forest crushed them. They were crushed under the weight of its changeless centuries. Their eyes and hearts grew weary—weary of those perpendicular lines receding in endless array—column after column of awful loftiness—and the twilit spaces in between empty but for lianas hanging straight, like chains for pendent censers.

Upon their return to the river they came in for a certain disappointment. They found the *Clio* exactly where they had left her. It appeared that the attempt to extricate her had proved a complete fiasco. In place of tugs two miserable little river steamers had arrived; and so incompetently had they been handled that at the end of half an hour's manœuvring they had collided and drifted off down-stream in a more or less disabled condition. Harry had thereupon taken the motor-boat into Obydos, leaving an invitation to the professor to join him there in the afternoon.

The company looked at one another. They felt that their expectations of release had been singularly naïve. Of course, this was the way things happened in Brazil; and not even the imposing Harry could make it otherwise.

As the day wore on the *Clio's* bower of snaky roots, writhing branches and long dark glossy leaves became ever more wearisomely familiar. The situation had lost its novelty, and the morning's walk had deprived the surrounding country of the glamour which attaches to the completely unknown. They now had a mental picture of what lay behind the river's green frontage. They could summon up a vision of grey silent solitudes stretching monotonously in every direction, with no passage through them except that by which the *Clio* had come—the five hundred miles of yellow water pouring down to the sea.

Man and man's works were dwarfed out of their true proportions; social questions had no importance here. It was difficult to regard the revolution as anything but a nuisance. To agitate politically in this country was simply to make oneself ridiculous in the face of nature.

As Mary leant over the rail first in one place and then in another, looking down at the yellow water, the glistening roots, and the small green crabs; staring through the boughs at the long desolate reach of the river; or plunging her gaze into the tangle of the forest;—as she stood passive to the influence of the place, she sank under a peculiar spell, she received a revelation, indefinite but deep. The most disturbing of its effects on her was the feeling that she could not, after all, marry Gerald. The forest insisted upon it. She argued with herself. She still wanted to find her own reason. The nearest she got to it was this: Gerald didn't see or feel the most important things. Those things were not merely ignored by him in the commotion of his outward existence; they lay beyond his perception. His love of life had seemed to match hers; they had shared so many enjoyments together; but now she understood that what he took pleasure in was *his own* vitality alone, not the vitality of the whole living earth—the spirit which expresses itself in the great silences of the earth's great wildernesses no less clearly than in the noise of aeroplane engines and jazz bands.

Harry and the professor came back in the evening just before dinner.

"Whew!" Harry dropped into a deck-chair and

mopped his forehead. "A pretty strenuous time we've been having—eh, professor? But the meeting couldn't have gone off better. Tremendous enthusiasm! As for organisation—well, that'll come—in time."

"I'm so glad!" said Lady Oswestry. "And *we* shall get away, I suppose—in time."

"Oh!" cried Harry, slapping his knee. "Not the slightest difficulty about that. A couple of proper tugs in the hands of experienced men will do it in five minutes. Those boats they sent this morning were a joke—a positive joke."

"Well," put in Sir James with gentleness, "might I ask, when will the tugs come?"

"The tugs," returned Harry, "they will be here upon my word of command."

"Then would you mind giving your word of command, Harry dear?" said his mother persuasively.

Harry was silent. He was drinking a gin-sling.

Hugo looked him up and down sardonically and then emitted a laugh.

Having put down his glass, Harry fixed his brother with a haughty regard. Indeed, as he leant back in his seat his air was so majestic that Sir James could not forbear to exclaim: "By gad! tugs or no tugs, Prince Florizel of Bohemia would have looked a mere gutter-snipe beside you, Harry!"

"My dear James!" Harry threw out a deprecating hand. "And yet," he murmured, looking down with modesty, "I must admit it—nature, without doubt, intended me to be a potentate."

Everybody laughed excepting the professor, who

pulled his beard thoughtfully. Sir James noticed this and said in an aside:

"Well, professor?"

There was a moment's hesitation; then, drawing his chair closer, the professor whispered:

"In confidence—I say it in confidence—last night, at the meeting, several voices did in fact acclaim him future Emperor of Amazonia."

Sir James drew in a long breath, turned and looked at Harry, then back at the professor again. Before he found his tongue Harry had again taken up speech:

"Ladies and gentlemen, let me lay before you the exact position of affairs at this moment. You remember I mentioned last night that one of the river monitors at Manaos had resisted our blandishments, remained faithful to the Federal Government, and steamed off down the river. Well, that ferocious little craft—the *Tigre* by name—has been firing at anything and everything on the way. Our commander abstained from going in immediate pursuit because he judged it necessary to give the officers and crews of the other ships a banquet to celebrate their espousal of our cause. The *Tigre* has, accordingly, a considerable start. It is not unlikely that she will arrive at Obydos to-morrow, run the gauntlet of the fire from our forts, and continue down-stream, hoping to escape into the Atlantic north of Marajo. I have therefore judged it wiser to leave the *Clio* in her present inconspicuous berth for the present. To tow her out would be tantamount to inviting the *Tigre* to sling a few shells at her as she went by."

"Well! you know best, Harry dear," said Lady

Oswestry after an expressive silence. And the dumbness of the others seemed to indicate that they were in a similarly resigned frame of mind. Their dumbness contained at any rate the tacit admission that Harry was the only one of the party who laid claim to knowing anything at all about revolutions and river-monitors and suchlike things. The glances exchanged, the eyebrows raised, were confessions of perfect helplessness.

Francis was the first to find his voice. He suggested that those parts of the *Clio* which were visible from the river should be camouflaged by painting them in green spots. But Lady Oswestry said drily that she wouldn't hear of it.

"Won't it be thrilling to-morrow," exclaimed Mary, "to think that at any moment we may be shelled!"

"We shall receive warning," said Harry, "from the guns in the forts at Obydos. Everyone who wants to will have time to take refuge on shore. My own opinion is, however, that you will all be safer here than anywhere else. For according to telegrams received the *Tigre* has not yet succeeded once in hitting the object she aimed at."

Again there was a meditative pause. Then Harry shifted his position and announced briskly: "To-morrow morning I shall have to go in to Obydos again. There is to be a gathering of the native chiefs of the district. And I have promised to give them a short address."

"What about?" asked Lady Oswestry faintly.

"That depends upon the temper of the meeting. I may discourse upon the iniquity of all forms of taxation; I may talk about the habits of the turtle and the cultivation of cassava; or again I may merely speak a few simple words about death and glory."

"In what language?"

"In Tupi."

Lady Oswestry knit her brows. "In what?"

"My dear mother," returned Harry loftily, "I said 'In Tupi'—and why not? There are only thirty-six words in the Tupi language, and I may tell you that I have mastered them all."

The professor opened his mouth, but it was only to emit a little cough of embarrassment.

"Harry!" cried Stella, "do—oh, do, take me in to Obydos with you to-morrow."

And somewhat to everyone's surprise, Harry said he would.

Chapter 16

THAT evening Sir James was the last to turn in. The night was clear and windless. High overhead shone the moon, casting flecks of light through the foliage on to the *Clio's* deck. A dark fretwork of leafy boughs patterned the silver of the river. The frogs were silent; the air was empty of all sound excepting the thin hum of the mosquitoes. Fever? said Sir James to himself, and gave a shrug. He did not care. Perhaps he had a touch of fever already. He was under the spell of an unaccountable exhilaration. He was possessed by a strange deep amusement. At what? At life. At the ridiculous, exciting, unimportant adventure of life.

A little later, on his way to bed, his ears caught the sound of talking and laughing in the cabin that Mary and Angela were sharing together. A smile flitted over his face as he strolled by. Sitting in the draught between his window and his open door, he mused and, unconsciously, he listened. Presently one of the girls came out. It would be Angela, he imagined, going to fetch something from her cabin. After a minute he rose, sauntered down the passage, and stopped outside Angela's doorway. Through the drawn curtain there came an odd, scuffling noise, and then he heard Angela swearing vigorously to herself.

"Hullo, Angela?" he called. "What's the matter, my dear?"

"Oh, Sir James, come in!" Angela's voice sounded agonised. "Come quick, for God's sake!"

He went in. The cabin was still all awry, with furniture piled up on the bed to get it out of the way. And, much to his astonishment, on the top of this pile he beheld Angela herself, precariously perched.

She was clinging and crouching there with her head right up against the ceiling, whilst her eyes were fixed in unfeigned alarm upon a spot in the centre of the floor.

"That animal there! Look! What is it? Take it away!" Her cry rang with hysterical fervour.

Sir James looked. It was certainly a very unprepossessing animal.

"Humph!" he temporised. "Is it a snake, an insect, or a fish?"

"How should I know?" returned Angela frantically. "Only, I implore you, take it away!"

"I think," said Sir James after a brief pause, "I think it would interest the professor." And he made a movement of withdrawal.

"No, no! For pity's sake," cried Angela, "don't leave me! These things are crumbling. I may slip down any minute. And just now it jumped at me."

"I have been told that some Brazilian frogs are as big as footballs," said Sir James. "And I imagine they go through a correspondingly large and unpleasant tadpole stage. In my opinion that is no more than a Brazilian tadpole."

"I've told you already," protested Angela with

heat, "that I don't care a *damn* what it is. I only beseech you to take it away."

Sir James looked round and then sidled along to the divan upon which there stood an open workbox. After tipping the contents out he advanced cautiously upon the animal and clapped the box down over it.

"Oh, splendid! Thanks awfully!" cried Angela in an ecstasy of relief.

Sir James looked up with a self-appreciatory smile. Then: "Wait a minute," he said quickly. "Don't attempt to come down yet. Your dress is caught."

Angela, who had already slid a few inches floorwards, arrested her descent. It was quite evident that what he said was true.

"I shall have to hoist you up a bit," said Sir James, coming beneath her. "You mustn't tear that frock. It's too pretty."

He did his best, no doubt, but their combined efforts were not successful. Angela's short skirt remained hitched up behind, and her new position was less decorous than before.

"Gracious heavens!" she murmured, with a confusion for which there was every excuse. "This is awful!"

"I think," said Sir James with detachment, "I think you would do well to rest upon my shoulder for a moment. Yes—like that. Now the strain is off the material."

He had only to turn his face a couple of inches to touch with his lips a little patch of smooth, white skin that appeared where the stocking ended. The next moment he went on:

"Now perhaps you can unhitch the skirt. But there's no hurry."

"This is too awful!" whispered Angela, glancing towards the door.

"We should hear if anyone were coming," replied Sir James reassuringly.

"I'm uncaught now," she went on after a final wriggle. "Please let me down—quick! You know, this is . . . this is really——"

Sir James took another deliberate kiss, then swung her down to the floor. Quite rosy, Angela stood with eyes downcast.

"I don't think you ought," she murmured reproachfully, "not a second time."

Sir James took her in his arms. "You're a dear child," he said. And during the next half-hour, after he had locked the door, he found her of an exquisite docility.

Yes, later, too, as he was reviewing the episode, Angela found credit in his eyes for a great deal of tact as well. She had affected neither brazenness nor prudery. She had not been absolutely frigid, nor had she simulated passion. In a word, she had played to perfection the rôle of *la petite fille* to his *bon papa*.

Lying awake in the dark damp heat, he reflected that it would certainly be amusing to marry her. The acquisition of this young slip of femininity should prove simple enough—hardly more disturbing than the purchase of a lovely Persian cat. It should decorate instead of destroy his bachelorhood. Angela was exactly fitted for the part. A level head, no temperament, no nerves, a strong constitution, and

an untiring devotion to externals. No hysterics, no
ill-health, no falling in love, no mystic yearnings,
to be apprehended. It would be enough that he
should impress upon her the fact that, as his wife,
she must not overstep a certain mark. Nor must she
run into debt—nor accept money from other men.
Fortunately she was extremely clever at dressing;
she made a little go a long way—necessity had taught
her, poor darling! Besides, dressmakers would be
prepared to equip her almost for nothing—just for
the sake of the advertisement. He could see that
as his wife she would find splendid scope for her
natural gifts. Of course, that would be her reason
for marrying him. To show herself off was all she
lived for. And he, for his part, wasn't asking for
anything more than the privilege of enjoying her
private, as well as her public, decorative effects.
Could any marriage be more suitable?

Old age lay ahead, it was true. And you couldn't
fancy Angela playing the hospital nurse or tending
a bedridden senility. No, whilst Marion offered true
companionship coupled with material comfort, Angela
was without anything but her finished and perfected
vapidity. He thought of his deathbed with a smile.
All he would require of her would be that she should
come in and display her new frock before going off
to some party. . . .

Still smiling, he propped himself up on one elbow
and took a long drink of iced water. Then as he
lay back he heard his first howling monkey. Coming
out of the thick, black, savage night, the sound had
a truly awesome quality. Bestially angry, bestially
melancholy, was that blend of a howl and a roar.

Other monkeys presently joined in. Scattered over the whole Amazonian forest, he supposed, these half human creatures were thus greeting a new day. It was at dawn they howled. For thousands and thousands of years they had thus howled; and they would thus howl for how many thousands of years to come?

It was so hot that the sweat trickled down his temples, but his mouth was parched as with fever. "Can no one tell me what they howl? Perhaps the plaintive numbers flow——" Good God, how idiotic! He was half dreaming; he seemed to see the monkeys in the tree-tops, their wizened faces turned to the East, watching dawn struggle through the sodden blankets of mist. Did the howling assuage a dim primeval anguish?

The uproar stopped as suddenly as it had begun; and then, patter, patter, patter—again the swiftly gathering rustle of rain. It developed into a deluge; and it continued.

Chapter 17

RAIN, indeed, was to be an almost constant feature of the remaining days of the *Clio's* captivity. Those days made their imprint upon the memory of everyone on board, not merely as days of calamity but also by reason of their excessive tediousness. Tedium and discomfort were ills that Lady Oswestry's guests were poorly equipped to bear. Of the two they bore discomfort the more bravely. One can make a joke of one's miseries, but boredom is always a bore.

Heavy and stagnant was the air of their prison under the trees. The mud stank; the trees dripped; insects swarmed. The damp brought mould out upon your shoes, almost liquefied the sugar and salt, and made everything clammy to the touch; the heat kept you busy wiping away rivulets of perspiration that trickled down your arms, down your legs, and down your forehead into your eyes. All day long wasps and flies plagued you with a varied buzzing; and in the night mosquitoes, rubbing their persistent noses against your curtain, kept up a more delicate hum. Maddening became the drip, drip, drip of the big, dark leaves upon the deck; and just when you were going to sleep, the monkeys started, or else it was the silly clamour of a million frogs.

All this was bad enough, but it mattered less than

time's awful drag. One seemed to be ordering one's existence by the hands of a clock that registered one hour when two must really have gone by. It was hopeless to attempt distraction involving intellectual effort. In this intense damp, in this intense heat, the mind was even less serviceable than the body.

Looks of positive detestation were cast at Joachim and Joao as they lolled happily about. What was time to them? They had no more sense of time, no more capacity for boredom, than the crocodile sunning himself upon the mud-flat.

No! As the doctor sardonically observed, to be bored is the privilege and distinction of the civilised man. If the more intelligent among the townsmen of Obydos were impelled by curiosity to sit all day in canoes under the downpour in order to stare at the *Clio*, the large majority were quite content to sit in their hammocks at home, staring at nothing at all.

Had they known beforehand how long their detention was to last, the strain upon the party would have been less severe. But every day brought forth fresh hopes which some accident presently dashed to the ground. At first the delay was directly attributable to the dilatoriness and inefficiency of the authorities at Obydos, but later it owed its cause to a tiresome mishap. The *Tigre*, after slipping by in the night without the firing of a single shot, ran aground on an island a couple of miles below the *Clio*; and as her guns commanded the only navigable waterway, traffic up and down the river was brought to a standstill.

Day after day Harry came out with the announcement that parleyings were in progress, and that should the *Tigre* continue obdurate, she would be shelled into submission. But in the meantime the rain persisted, the forest steamed, the heat abated not, and nearly everyone on board began to feel out of sorts.

Sir James, indeed, after his night spent in listening to the howling monkeys, felt quite distinctly ill. Of this he said nothing, however; if he betrayed himself at all it was by an unwonted captiousness. During the course of the morning he seriously ruffled Mr. Wilkinson. But their argument was cut short by Harry who came into the saloon accompanied by three or four of the crew heavily laden with packages.

After these had been set down Harry turned to the women of the party, who were sitting together in one corner. "There!" said he. "Now you can do your shopping here in comfort. These boxes contain samples of everything that Obydos can provide."

When the lid of the first box was lifted Angela gave a cry of delight.

"Oh, look! How divine!"

Mr. Wilkinson, who could see well enough from where he sat, immediately turned red in the face. The box contained aigrettes.

He rose and advanced upon the ladies. He spoke; but not one of them had any attention to spare. Baffled, he wheeled round in search of a supporter and caught in Sir James's eye a faint but unmistakable gleam of mockery.

He returned; he stood over the cynic, glaring.

"And those," he spluttered, "those are people whom you, I believe, consider civilized!"

With that he marched out of the room.

Sir James, now beaming with open amusement, addressed himself to the doctor, who had just come in.

"Did you hear that?" he exclaimed. "Dear Mr. Wilkinson! His feelings do him credit. I swear they do!"

"Then why don't you share them?"

"Because I have the sense to see that sentiment misapplied spoils itself and its object. I prefer *not* to sugar my oysters."

The doctor expressed some sympathy with Mr. Wilkinson's views.

"Tut, tut!" replied Sir James. "The white heron is of course a lovely creature, but it has no better claim to humanitarian consideration than the chicken which Mr. Wilkinson ate at lunch yesterday. Don't tell me that it is not as necessary for a pretty woman to have an aigrette in her hat as for Mr. Wilkinson to have a wing of chicken in his stomach. I consider it much more necessary—and more important. Far greater issues depend on it."

"All the same," objected the doctor, "I believe that women nowadays are giving up the wearing of feathers."

"That," returned Sir James, "indicates no more than a passing change of fashion or opinion, not a change of heart. No! if I thought that the admonishments of my friend, Mr. Wilkinson, were likely to change women's hearts I should be plunged into despair. But history offers no grounds for the belief that human nature ever will change—at any rate for what Mr. Wilkinson would call the better. That is the one and only happy conclusion to be drawn from the recent war."

The doctor smiled indulgently, letting this *boutade* pass.

"The gastronomic appeal of roast chicken," continued Sir James, "is far grosser than the æsthetic appeal of an aigrette in the hat of——"

"Oh, come!" protested the doctor mildly. "Do you call that an *æsthetic* appeal?"

Sir James smiled. "No matter. Another line of argument will do equally well. Talking to a female psycho-analyst the other day, I said in order to provoke her, 'You bring everything down to sex.' '*Up* to sex,' she retorted, and I confess I found nothing to reply."

Very slowly did that day wear on while the rain came down unceasingly. It was not until sundown that the sky cleared, ushering in a limpid, rose-tinted evening. In couples the prisoners on the *Clio* came out and paced the deck. The air, however, was so heavy that after a few minutes their briskness degenerated into languor, and finally they stood leaning over the rail, too limp to do more than stare dreamily at a scene they already knew far too well.

As the moon came up the rosy tints of river and sky were changed to silver. It was a moment of exquisite beauty. Hugo, as he gazed, felt once again that for his part he would be content to spend a month, perhaps a year, at Obydos—but without the

Clio, without society—living the life of a savage—fishing, hunting, gazing mindlessly at the changing colours of dawn and evening.

Whilst he was thus dreaming clouds rolled up, the moon was shrouded, darkness fell. With a sigh he moved to the other side of the deck. Beams of yellow light struck out from the portholes below; and he noticed that upon every root on which the light happened to fall scores of little crabs had collected, and there clung staring with beady eyes at the ship.

"Disgusting little creatures!" murmured Hugo.

The doctor, who was near by, grunted a vague assent. For some minutes they both stared back at the crabs in silence; then Hugo asked:

"How is the captain? How are all your patients?"

The doctor pursed his lips. It was an open secret that there were a good many cases of sickness among the personnel. The captain, he replied slowly, was doing pretty well; but Harrison, the steward, unquestionably had blackwater fever. And then: "It can't be denied," he went on, "this spot is infernally unhealthy. The last man to go down on my sick-list is Sir James."

"Oh!" Hugo looked round sharply. "What's the matter with him?"

The doctor kept his eyes fixed upon the crabs.

"I can't say yet," was his answer. And Hugo felt a sudden sinking of the heart.

All the evening he brooded. He realised better than ever before how deep his attachment to Sir James was. Sympathy had sprung up between them years ago when no one but Sir James saw anything in him but the stiff, priggish schoolboy that he was. Nor had he been slow to discover *l'homme de cœur* in Sir James—although few others believed such a man to exist beneath the worldly exterior.

For most of the night Hugo lay awake, restless as much from anxiety as from physical discomfort. Once or twice he got up and listened outside Sir James's door. All was silent inside. He could not guess that the sick man was deliberately renouncing even the relief of an occasional groan.

Sir James had no liking for pity. The next day he allowed no one to stay in his cabin for long, because he would not permit an expression of suffering to be seen upon his face. Although the night had been a long-drawn torture, he preferred it to the daytime; at night others were asleep and would not visit him—asleep and therefore not even thinking about him.

In the evening, however, he sent for Hugo.

"It's quite possible," said he, "that nothing is seriously amiss with me; but in this country you never know. The partition between life and death is as thin as the paper wall of a Japanese house. A stumble sends one through it. If you don't mind, my dear boy, I will ask you to act as my secretary for an hour or so."

That night Sir James's sufferings became so acute that he actually longed for death. What a relief it would be to die before day came! What a relief to be dispensed from composing one's face, and answering questions, and behaving decently. Nothing was expected of a dead man—lucky fellow! He could rot in peace.

At dawn the monkeys began howling; and they must have been closer to the ship than ever before, for the noise they made was blood-curdling. It was almost unbelievable that so insignificant an animal could produce such a volume of sound—a noise that united the bellow of a bull with the howl of a wounded tigress. Sir James welcomed the uproar. It drowned the exasperating song of the mosquitoes.

As the light increased the air grew cooler and his distress was somewhat mitigated. He took heart from the thought that after all it would not cost him too terrible an effort to conduct himself as he wished. To make a start he dragged his aching body from the bed; and, although he could hardly sit upright, he managed to shave.

A little later the doctor came in. Sir James waited till he had made his examination, then he said:

"My dear McLaren, don't imagine that you can tell me anything I don't already know. It's pretty plain now—what I'm suffering from—blackwater fever. And I know how that ends."

"There is another man on board who has had all your symptoms," replied the doctor, "and now he is on the road to recovery."

Sir James closed his eyes. "That young fellow is my junior by about thirty-five years," said he.

The doctor gave him an opiate, and then at his request left him. Sir James wanted to contemplate his position quietly. "Dying is a lonely business," said he to himself; "but then so is being alive."

As he lay in bed, watching the light increase and

listening to the morning clamour of the frogs, he wondered whether his remaining span of life would be twenty-four, thirty-six, or forty-eight hours. Although his mind was serene, his heart was contracted and chilled by an instinctive abhorrence of death. "This shrinking is coeval with life," he reflected. "I inherit it from the amœba. But reason, although it can do little to make living less difficult, ought at least to make dying easy. Let me remember that to a deep sleeper one second and eternity are the same."

These reflections did not, however, prevent recurrent spasms of rebellion and dread. It was a trifle, generally, that set him off—for instance, the thought that it was now a matter of no consequence on what day his shirts would return from the ship's laundry. Although he was able to confront death without terror whenever he made the necessary effort, he found it impossible to keep his mind permanently keyed up to the realisation that he was going to die. Frequent were his lapses into semi-forgetfulness. And then followed the jar of reawakened realisation and the instinctive sinking of the heart.

It gave him pleasure to consider how carefully he had settled his affairs; friends, relatives and servants had all alike received their due. Just as no one could say that during his lifetime he had been slipshod and inefficient, so no one would have just cause to reproach him after death. He had no accounts to settle with anyone. His flirtation with Angela had, luckily, not gone far enough to give her, or anyone else, the right to attach importance to it. There was no one whom he need see again—except

Marion. She was no doubt a little piqued; but it was easy to forgive a dying man. If he alluded to Angela at all, it would be with a lightness that might well do a little to enliven the rather dreary business of bidding her goodbye.

The news of Sir James's illness had caused less stir on board than might have been expected. The reason was that in this country to be ill seemed more natural than to be well; and as for dying, even that no longer appeared to be such a tremendous affair. Very swiftly do the tropics instil a certain measure of fatalism. Everyone said that, of course, Sir James would soon be better; but after the second day of his illness not a soul on board believed it.

The person to make the most to-do was Francis. Fastening upon whoever he could, he would pour forth in a torrent of grave, low, rapid speech warnings, criticisms, prognostications and advice. Was Dr. McLaren really doing all that could be done? Was the disease likely to spread? Didn't you think that . . . ? Wasn't it odd that . . . ? Oughtn't so-and-so to be told that . . . ? etc. But no one gave him much encouragement. His resistance to the ethos of the place was judged remarkable. After listening to him for twenty minutes Mr. Wilkinson and the professor agreed that triviality carried to such a pitch was indicative of unusual vitality. Francis was both negligible and extraordinary.

Sir James's character incidentally came in for a good deal of discussion.

"He has stoicism," said the professor.

"He is vain, selfish and unprincipled," said Mr. Wilkinson. "His feelings have atrophied. It is not difficult to be stoical when you have nothing to live for."

If Mr. Wilkinson was severe upon Sir James it was partly because he was jealous of the latter's influence over Hugo. Besides, he did not yet realise how ill Sir James was. He was always slow to believe that a member of the ruling caste might be in a position calling for commiseration. Over the seaman, Harrison, he had expended much anxious sympathy; while the man's life was in danger he had considered the party most insufficiently concerned. But about Sir James he felt more or less indifferent. It did not occur to him that in this he was exhibiting the same characteristic as Francis to whom even a cold in the head seemed important if it chanced to affect a personage such as Sir James, while Harrison's death would have left him unmoved.

Mr. Wilkinson, like Sir James, had reached the age to take an interest in the tendencies of the rising generation. He would have liked to become Hugo's mentor, not only because he looked upon him as a promising young man, but because the middle-aged can find no assurance of the worth or permanence of their ideas except in the minds of the young. Considering himself progressive, Mr. Wilkinson expected to receive this assurance, and was ill-pleased when he found Hugo maintaining his allegiance to a less enlightened contemporary.

Of the two characters Hugo certainly admired Sir James's the more, chiefly because Sir James's standards were the more dignified. The honour of the human race was safer in that man's hands, his selfishness, hardness, and cynicism notwithstanding.

He had an intuition that Sir James's materialism was impregnated with idealism, while the concealed foundations of Mr. Wilkinson's idealism were, he judged, materialistic. The little books of essays about Love, Truth, and Beauty, written by Mr. Wilkinson and his friends, conveyed no meaning to him whatsoever. A far deeper devotion to the things of the spirit was implicit in one page of Nietzsche.

He liked Mr. Wilkinson well enough, but Sir James he loved. His rapidly gathering conviction that Sir James would not recover filled his heart with grief.

Chapter 18

DURING these days he had been waiting with impatience for an opportunity to see something more of the forest. On several occasions he had made a start, but the heavy rain, the thick mists, and the swampy condition of the ground had always forced him back. Now at last, however, after a night without rain, the sun was rising clear and bright. He determined forthwith to set out. His desire to explore was reinforced by an even greater longing for solitude.

For about an hour he went forward over familiar ground; then, for another hour, through a region similar in aspect, but unreached before. The monotony of the scenery was growing wearisome, when he descried at no great distance ahead a long low ridge; and it seemed to him that beyond it the forest had a different character. Wherein the difference lay was not easy to determine. Perhaps it was only a modification of the lighting. But what caused that change?

He made his way up the gentle slope and on reaching the top stood still in astonishment. A sheet of coal-black water stretched away before him. The huge trunks of the trees were reflected downwards to the same distance as they towered above. It was a forest built upon a forest, and wherever

his gaze turned it lost itself in a grey-green
obscurity.

He reflected that this great flood was probably
more or less permanent. The professor had told
him that the numerous lakes in the vicinity spread
out during many months of the year, bringing immense
tracts of low lying forest under water. The scene
which lay before his eyes might be extended by the
imagination over hundreds of square miles. In these
regions there would be no life excepting that of
fishes, frogs, and snakes. The monkeys and birds
dwelt far out of sight above. This was the domain of
dull cold-blooded things. He could picture the huge
anaconda swimming stealthily through the gloom.
He saw the monster hardly rippling the glassy, black
water as it moved; but ever and again it would lift
its head while its lidless eyes searched for prey. By
the scanty light of the sun and by the scantier light
of the moon the creatures of the region carried on
their silent, furtive, greedy life. But, in the main,
these waters, everlastingly shaded, slept a sleep that
was unbroken by any animal sound or stir. They
looked indeed as if they lay under the spell of a
complete stagnancy. The winds above might blow,
but hardly a breath would penetrate here; the rain
might fling itself down in torrents, but with no
effect beyond putting the glister of running wet upon
the tree-trunks and punctuating the stillness here
and there with a big, heavy drip.

Hugo sat himself down and stared vacantly. On
board the *Clio* Angela would be stitching at a pink
chemise, Simpson was probably taking a whisky
and soda, Stanford was poring over some differential

equation, and Sir James was sinking to his death. How transitory did that scene appear when compared with this which had not changed since the building of the Pyramids and would still be the same after the *Clio* and her company had turned to dust. "Alas," thought Hugo, "it is the mind that perishes, and the works of the mind that moth and rust do corrupt. Time is only set at nought where it is not known; the sting of death is reserved for man alone. I, in self-consciousness, sit here and suffer because I know that the life of the wisest man on earth is agitated, vain and brief."

With these reflections he sank into utter despondency. Sir James, his dearest friend, was dying; Stella, his mistress, was casting him off. He felt bereft, diminished, of nothing worth. The sombreness, the awfulness, of the forest sank into him; he sat hypnotised and crushed; his spirit writhed in the dust.

How long this agonising stupor lasted he could not have said. But there came a moment when, tortured beyond endurance, he sprang to his feet and hurried with stumbling steps along the margin of the flooded aisles. As he proceeded in this new direction the character of the forest changed. The trees, less dense above, admitted of undergrowth. Bushes and saplings obstructed his way; there was a greater abundance of lianas and trailing vines; it was not long before he found himself struggling through a veritable jungle. To force a passage he was obliged to make use of the hatchet which Joachim had advised him to take. His progress was now very slow, but he laboured on, at first because the exercise distracted him from his thoughts, and then, later, because he descried, not far ahead, patches of brightness which could be nothing else but the glitter of actual sunlight. In his eyes, accustomed as he now was to a semi-obscurity, that distant glitter looked harsh and artificial. But it drew him on; and a few minutes later he came out into a well of scorching heat and blinding radiance, a small circular glade recently caused by the overthrow of several giant trees blown down in a hurricane. The rich, damp ground was already green with sprouting vegetation. Across it ran a trickle of water half lost in mosses, ferns and grasses. Pools, some shallow, some apparently deep, reflected the white-hot sky. These pools were rimmed with a light green scum upon which rested enormous butterflies that were slowly opening and shutting their black and yellow wings. Above the water were suspended striped dragon-flies of equally monstrous size. For some minutes he stood staring from the edge of the forest. Of all the lush green things sprouting up in the fiery sunlight, not one tree, not one weed, was familiar. The scene wore in his eyes an aspect of sinister unreality.

At last he went forward and stood by the margin of the nearest pool. His feet moved noiselessly on the carpet of moss, but all at once a decaying twig broke with a sharp crack beneath his tread. The next instant the glassy surface of the water was broken into a hundred intersecting ripples. Gazing intently, he caught a glimpse of flat heads and mottled bodies sliding out of the warm, stagnant water into the thickness of the weeds. Hugo had a hatred of snakes and knew that the *jararaca*, the most poisonous species in Brazil, abounded in jungle pools. Shuddering, he took an incautious step to the rear and the next instant felt something writhe beneath his foot. Before he had time even to look down he received a tiny stab. What had bitten him? Could it have been anything other than a *jararaca*? Immediately the whole world darkened to his vision, the sweat upon his heated body seemed to turn to ice. With limbs that quaked, and with a burning head, he picked his way back to the verge of the forest and there sat down to examine the bite. Two tiny drops of blood stained his white sock, and in the skin underneath were two small bluish punctures. He squeezed them, and with inward loathing applied his mouth to the place where the creature had struck. Having sucked, he vomited; rage, disgust, and the fear of death mingling in an indescribable nausea. He had forgotten to bring his packet of permanganate of potash, so beyond making a tight ligature above the bite with his handkerchief, there was nothing he could do. In the awful stillness of the place he groaned aloud. "I shall die here," he thought, "and I pray to God that my poisoned, swollen, discoloured corpse may never be found."

But after he had lain upon the ground for a few minutes his horror of the place became so acute that he started up. Stay here! Die here! By God! he would not. At the risk of driving the poison over his body he would make an attempt to regain the ship. At the worst, death in the grey gloom of the forest would be preferable to death in this green and glittering hell.

Heedless now of thorns, stinging ants and flies,

he took what he judged to be the most direct route to the ship, and plunged violently forward. To erase all thought from his mind was now his chief desire. Nor was he wholly unsuccessful, for before very long he sank into a feverish stupor. After covering about two miles he tried to reckon how much time had gone by since he was bitten. His foot was numb; but he was still practically without pain.

As the ground became clearer he was able to proceed more rapidly. He was unconscious of fatigue; waves of hope surged over his heart.

When, however, he had put another couple of miles behind him he realised that he should already have struck across his former path or at least be able to recognise some of the distinguishing features of the ground. But nothing, alas, was familiar; he searched in vain for a landmark. A new terror descended upon him. He could not resist the conviction that he had gone astray. He was lost.

Brought to a halt he closed his eyes, and stood swaying like one about to faint. Exhaustion—a stupefying mental and physical exhaustion—overcame him. He staggered to the nearest tree and lay down, his back against the trunk. Then suddenly he became aware—appallingly aware—of a dull ache in his foot. The next instant lightning pains shot up his leg. Again he closed his eyes.

This then was the end . . . the end of a futile life. He didn't care. Except, alas, for his mother! There was no one else. Not Stella, no. She wouldn't care. Nor Harry particularly; nor Stanford with his mathematics; nor Angela with her pink chemises;

nor Mary, who had her Gerald. Human relationships! Did they really count for much? Olga? She might be a little sorry. But to her he was indifferent. As for his career—what did that matter? Did anything matter then? Ah yes! Life! To live! To be alive! It was wonderful beyond words. He saw that now. Now that he was already dead. He would keep his eyes shut till the end came. He had no wish to see the light again.

Darkness! Silence! Time was passing. Let it pass! Let him forget the world of movement, talk and laughter—forget the small daily joys of being alive. He wished that the birds so high overhead would be silent. What was that falling through the branches? A dead bough, or a nut dropped by a monkey. Again a sound—like a dry twig breaking. But he refused to open his eyes—never again. He was too weary. . . .

Nevertheless his lids did part slowly, and slowly his vision of the forest returned. Again those grey aisles, hoary, dim, boundless, desolate, and yet—there in the distance something white was moving. He started and stared. It was a human figure—a girl in white, Mary!

A shudder passed over him. The change of feeling was too violent to be joyful. He felt humiliated and confused. Only a child can swallow its grief and pass in one second, unresentfully, from misery into joy. Hugo's expression as he stared at Mary, was almost one of anger. The world of illusion, the world of reality—which was which? To behold the girl strolling unconcernedly along, not two hundred yards from the spot where he lay lost and dying—it was

an outrage. He prayed she might not see him. He
pressed close to the root-buttress of his tree. She
looked so collected, so serene, so fresh, too, in her
white dress. Illusion! Reality! They jostled each
other in a mind which could no longer distinguish
between them. Soul-racking illusion! Trivial, mocking reality! He was the plaything of both. Here he
lay still in pain, still utterly exhausted, still sick from
the strain of his recent experiences. And yet—was
he really in pain? Was his exhaustion genuine?
Had any of his experiences been less than half
illusory?

As Mary drew nearer he trembled still more lest
she should catch sight of him. How should he
explain himself? In these moments he no longer
feared but hoped that it was a *jararaca* that had
bitten him. His amour-propre imperiously demanded
that he should suffer an immediate and painful death.
Was she going to pass unseeing? Alas, no! Her
gaze strayed in his direction; with a cry of surprise
and a smile of greeting she turned her steps towards
him. He lacked the spirit to do so much as stir.
He did not even attempt to produce an answering
smile. In misery he waited for the change that
would appear upon her face when she was near enough
to notice his condition—the marks of his bodily and
moral distress.

Yes, here it was! Her looks altered. "Hugo!"
she cried out, her voice expressive of consternation.
She broke into a run and flung herself down at
his feet.

She questioned, but he could not command his
voice sufficiently to reply. Her solicitude, even

whilst he was inwardly raging against himself, made his eyes brim over from self-pity. "Purely reflex action!" he was longing to explain, but for the moment he could only blink.

"Hugo darling!" cried Mary with still deeper concern; and she made haste to produce her handkerchief. His tears had turned him into a little boy. Indeed, she would have wiped his eyes herself, had he not snatched the handkerchief from her with all a child's shamefaced pettishness.

"Hugo! what has happened to you?" she supplicated. "Oh, Hugo, tell me what to do!"

Her perfect simplicity, her abandonment, single-hearted, to the instinct of pity invested her, too, with a childlike quality. He dared to look up into her face, and in that moment he saw her with new eyes. He saw her as absolutely adorable. Whilst he gazed his lips quivered into a smile. Had he been capable of articulate utterance, he would not have scrupled to speak out from his heart. As it was, all he could do was to emit a thin, uncertain laugh.

She stared, bewildered. His white, haggard face, his bleeding hands and tattered clothing, contrasted strangely with this mirth. But the next instant the look in his eyes enlightened her. She understood. This was a kind of confession. He was laughing at himself. Nothing so very dreadful had really happened; it had *seemed* dreadful; but the nightmare had lifted.

She gave a divine smile; her sympathy was unchanged. It flowed in the same full stream to comfort the new Hugo that was revealed to her. If in the past she had stood a little in awe of him,

she now felt simply and solely that he was a poor
lamb deserving of all compassion. Whilst she murmured reassurances he looked at her in an ecstacy
of gratitude. He forgot his dignity. The story of
his tribulations came out haltingly, with sighs of
rueful amusement.

"But it *was* awful!" she cried. "You were right
to be terrified. The whole thing was too dreadful
for words."

She was so sincere, so unreserved in her generosity,
that Hugo's heart melted completely. Again he
found himself bereft of speech; but he seized her
hand and kissed it.

A moment of silence and shyness followed. Then
he attempted to rise, but at once sank backward to
the ground again with a wince of pain.

"Do you know!" he murmured in re-awakened
alarm, "my foot does, all the same, hurt me frightfully."

But Mary, who had been examining the foot, had
a diffident suggestion. "Don't you think it might
be because that handkerchief is tied so *very*
tight?"

After she had undone the knot, Hugo moved his
foot cautiously this way and that, and presently he
admitted that the pain was subsiding.

Not many minutes later they were walking, side
by side, back to the ship. Like Hugo, Mary was
now stricken with silence and not a little shy. But
in her heart a bewildered happiness reigned. Scarcely
did she dare to steal a glance at Hugo as he limped
along beside her. If, deep in her heart she rejoiced
to feel him her slave, in her mind she was over-

whelmed and embarrassed by the suddenness and importance of her capture.

Upon reaching the ship Hugo went straight to his cabin, threw himself upon the bed, and slept unbrokenly until evening. When he awoke it was to see his mother standing beside him. Smiling contentedly, he put out his hand. His sleep had been delicious; and he was thankful—oh, how thankful!—to be still in the world of the living.

But his mother's sad face brought back to him the memory of Sir James. He questioned her and learnt that Sir James was not expected to live through the night.

Chapter 19

SIR JAMES's last talk with Lady Oswestry took place a few hours later. His first words, when she came in, were to assure her that he was no longer in any pain. He even smiled as he spoke (it was evident that he shrank as much as ever from any display of emotion), but his face was so yellow and haggard that he looked a different man.

She sat down by the bed and took his hand in hers. Although her eyes were turned away, she was aware that his gaze was fixed intently upon her; and for the first time in her life she was not sorry that she was looking far from her best. What he would not let her say—what, maybe, he would only half believe if she said it—that she would allow her poor, sorrow-marked face to say for her. She let the light of the electric lamp fall full upon it—upon a face aged by grief, a devastated face, that art had not attempted to repair.

There was a brief silence. Then, without more than a flicker of her eyes, she interpreted the look which had crept over his countenance. She understood it to be the reflection of a secret, irrepressible content. "Ah," he was thinking, "perhaps she really did love me after all!" And she was happy to give him this proof patent of her grief.

He said: "Well, Marion dear, I don't think this

move of mine is altogether a bad one. You know,
I should have got very tired of myself as an old
man."

She let him continue on this note without attempting
a reply. The pressure of her hand sufficed him. He
went on speaking, but with frequent lapses into
silence. She could see that he was quite at his ease.
Presently he threw out: "Death saves one, you
know, from a multitude of follies!" And his smile
explained well enough what he meant.

"Marion," he said a little later, "I doubt whether
you realise how much you have been in my thoughts
during the twenty odd years that I've known you.
Your vitality, your courage, your never-failing
charm. . . ." His voice died away, but she
just caught the words "an inborn gallantry of
character."

To this again she said nothing. He should never
know that his tribute of praise fell upon a heart
bitter with despair. Her courage! Good God!
where was her courage now? Little did he realise
that she was passing through a spiritual ordeal no
less severe than his. For her the hour about to
strike was the hour not of bereavement only but
also of renunciation. She felt—and the persuasion
this time was irresistible—that her Indian summer
was drawing to a close. She might have told him
that he was luckier than she; for whilst he was
merely passing from waking into sleep, she was
slipping from Life into Death-in-Life. She was
entering the last stage of a woman's existence, when
she has to live unsupported by the expectation,
conscious or unconscious, of a love affair.

As if not wholly unaware of the trend of her thoughts, he said after a while:

"Marion, you will never grow old."

She closed her eyes and shook her head mutely.

"You have Hugo," he added. And a minute later he went on in a fainter voice. "I won't ask to see Hugo again. I'm too fond of him. You can tell him I said that."

She could see that he had grown very tired. His lids had dropped. She studied him a minute with passionate intensity, then rose and, bending, kissed him on the brow. He must have felt the tear which dropped upon his face, for he winced slightly. In a voice not quite under control he articulated: "Being dead may, after all, be less dull than I have always imagined." And opening his eyes he gave her a parting smile: "Perhaps it is au revoir, my dear," he said.

An hour later he fell into a semi-conscious state. Once or twice he muttered something about Angela, and then something about the howling monkeys. Whether he looked forward to the usual uproar at dawn, or whether he hoped to die first, was not easy to determine. At about two o'clock he surprised the doctor by concentrating his faculties sufficiently to frame one or two definite questions regarding the monkeys' appearance and habits. The doctor went to the professor's cabin and woke him to obtain the desired information. Returning, he said:

"The howling monkey stands about two feet high. He has long silky hair, of a reddish-brown colour on the back, golden on the flanks. It is owing to an unusual development of the hyoid bone that his cry has such extraordinary resonance. The howling

monkey can make himself heard easily at a distance
of two miles. When he howls he sits at the top of
some great tree which dominates the surrounding
forest."

"Thank you," breathed Sir James, who had
listened with a feeble smile. He died not long afterwards, just before the monkeys began their concert.

The next morning Francis and Angela were the
first on deck. Francis was in pyjamas, Angela had on
a black dress. "It's really an evening frock," she
explained. "Haven't I been clever in adapting it?"

"In this country," said Francis, "it is the fashion
for men to put on evening dress at funerals; but
really! . . ." And he flourished his amber cigarette-
holder.

Angela sighed and gazed out over the river with
pensive melancholy. She was aware that all the
sympathy on board was reserved for Lady Oswestry.
As for her own position, Sir James's death merely
brought her under ironical comment.

Francis prattled on:

"My headache to-day is something frightful.
Splitting, my dear, absolutely splitting! I was awake
all night thinking of poor Sir James. I am like that,
you know. I feel these things deeply. Besides, I
was simply devoted to the poor man. A wonderful
character! He was telling me all about himself only
the other evening. Poor darling Marion! I don't
know how she'll get over it. But really, you know,
he ought never to have come on this trip. A man of
that age. . . . It wasn't wise. I suppose you know
the funeral is to be this morning. One has to be very
quick in this climate. He's to be buried in the

forest. Do you realise how lucky it is that that
deck-hand didn't die ? We should have had to give
him a regular pompous ceremony ; the crew would
have expected it. You know what those people are !
And then it would have been very difficult to do less
for Sir James. As it is we can cut out all the plumes
and crape. Just a hole under the trees and a few
lines from the burial service. . . . He would have
hated anything more." And Francis sighed feelingly.

The interment took place in the afternoon. It
occupied the whole morning to dig a grave. There
was nothing remarkable about the site, which had
been chosen for reasons of convenience. In most
places digging was almost an impossibility owing to
the profusion, thickness and hardness of the tree roots.

Unfortunately news of the funeral had spread to
Obydos. Upon arriving at the grave Sir James's
friends found that a large crowd had already assembled
there. Not only were representatives of the civil
and military authorities present, but all the more
energetic inhabitants of the town had arisen from
their hammocks, donned their well-worn funeral
garb, and hastened to the spot. This was the kind
of function to which taste and habit most inclined
them. Besides, Sir James had been the personal
friend of that hero and up-to-date Lord Byron,
Harry.

The ceremony over, the rank and fashion of Obydos
moved on to their next entertainment, which had
been advertised as the shelling of the still recalcitrant
Tigre. In this case, however, they were destined
to suffer a disappointment. Just before the opening
of the proceedings the *Tigre* spontaneously blew up.

To the travellers on the *Clio* this fact announced itself by a violent detonation, the cause of which remained uncertain until Joachim, who had been out in a canoe, returned quivering with excitement and bubbling over with gruesome particulars. "Everything most 'orrible," he summed up with relish. "No more *Tigre* left. Peoples all in little bits. All bloody and 'orrible. You not like to come and see?"

Harry, Hugo and the doctor set out at once, taking all hands that could be spared, including two stewardesses who had had hospital training. The boats pushed off into the river under the red light of an unusually lurid sunset. The barometer was falling rapidly. Joachim predicted a storm from the west. "But only leetle storm," he added reassuringly. "Leetle wind, plenty rain, and much noise—boum, boum—in ze sky."

In silence the company hung over the rail watching the darkness fall. The sultriness increased; the electric tension of the atmosphere became almost unbearable. Sweat trickled down faces and limbs. One stood until tired of standing, then sat oneself under an electric fan and remained there, lax, with closed eyes, until a gnawing restlessness brought one again to the rail to stare at the coppery gloom of the sky, the darkening river, and the obscurity of the forest—the forest in which fire-flies, more numerous than usual, gave a hint of infinitely receding distances. There was nothing to mitigate the discomfort, the ennui, and the melancholy of this hour. No one mentioned Sir James. No one spoke of the funeral. But the picture of it lingered in every mind. Without

being in the least impressive, it had been somehow—
significant.

It was not until ten o'clock that the low moan of
tempest became audible. After that, affairs moved
rapidly. The frogs at once stopped croaking; a
puff of moist rain-scented air swept through the
trees, the water lapped briskly against the sides of
the ship; and then, after an interval that could be
reckoned in seconds, the *Clio* was in the midst of an
uproar. Rain poured in streams from the creaking,
struggling trees. Through their tough foliage the
wind made a rustling so prodigious that that sound
held its own against all others except the thunder
and an occasional crash signifying the fall of some
forest giant. As an example of one of nature's
tantrums the disturbance was awe-inspiring even to
the sheltered, snugly-housed occupants of the *Clio*.
The fury of the gale in the tree-tops was to be likened to
nothing but the battling of two hosts of aerial dragons.

For the greater part of the night the turmoil continued. It was not until four o'clock that sleep
became possible. When the *Clio's* company awoke,
however, it was to find the sun shining in a cloudless
sky, and the air tempered to a delicious freshness. So
cool was it that all remained in their cabins to a late
hour dozing away the weariness and fever of the night.

In the meantime Harry, Hugo and the doctor had
passed through many hours of hard toil and severe
discomfort. The storm had not only impeded the
extrication of the wounded from the shattered ship,
but had put a stop to their transference to Obydos.
It had been necessary to erect temporary shelters
upon the island itself. Hour after hour Hugo had

toiled. Hour after hour he had been the shrinking witness of suffering and death. But the pitiful confusion which the rescue party met with upon their arrival had gradually given place to order. Not long after dawn Hugo found himself at liberty to slip away.

In a canoe hired from a native he paddled himself gently towards the northern bank. His brain was dulled by fatigue; languor melted his very bones. He felt himself to be as passive a thing as the tufts of uprooted waterweed that went drifting by. Like them he was tossed up and down on the wavelets. Like an old board lying out in the sun, he gratefully absorbed the warmth that fell upon his back. His mind was fluid; his thoughts as changeful as mist wreaths; impressions, not vivid, but deep and dreamlike, flowed over him.

His lazy paddling brought him at last to the forest bank upon which the morning light fell golden. The foliage was glistening with wet. Moisture trickled down the hanging lianas and dripped into his passing canoe. Water-fowl dived and hid among the weeds. Lily leaves lay flat and clean upon the yellow water. Everywhere warmth and wet. And this was perpetual —one season hardly differing from another—and the years all the same.

Hugo gazed and brooded dreamily over what his eyes showed him. The stress and turmoil of the night had faded out of his consciousness. Indeed he was free of all memories, Mary herself being present in his mind not as an object of thought, but as the medium—a hazy golden medium—in which his dreams were floating.

After tying his canoe to an overhanging bough

he stretched out his limbs and fell into a doze. He might have remained there for hours had not the rising sun slanted its beams through the foliage right into his face. Gradually he roused himself, sat up, and looked around. The mists had lifted, and there in mid-stream, about a mile away, a smart, white ship was anchored. It took him at least a minute to realise that he was gazing at the *Clio*.

The pleasure of this surprise was tempered almost immediately by a feeling akin to regret. A page of life had been turned, bringing him unexpectedly to the end of the chapter. In many respects it had been a painful chapter; and yet now that it was finished he was not wholly glad.

Very different was the aspect which the *Clio* now presented. Her bows pointing downstream seemed ready to cut the water at any moment; smoke was pouring from her funnels; she looked once more her old energetic self. As he started paddling towards her, her whistle sounded three imperious blasts. He quickened his strokes. Already from this distance he could discern the bustle on board. A few minutes later he was able to make out Francis and Angela leaning over the rail. They waved to him; he could imagine their excited chatter.

Chapter 20

AFTER a hurried bath and a change of clothes Hugo joined the crowd under the awning. Harry and his party had returned an hour ago; the *Clio* had already made up steam; there was nothing to detain her. Very soon her whistle sounded again and she was off.

Delicious was the rush of air as she swept downstream against the breeze. The women's light skirts were moulded against their limbs; they had to cling to their hats; colour mounted into pale cheeks. Not even the thought of Sir James was able to subdue the general animation. Lady Oswestry, who had emerged from her cabin, was at pains not to display signs of grief. She was determined, as Hugo could see, that her presence should not act as a constraint.

An important ingredient in the general elation was the sense of an escape from alien subjection. The forest no longer lorded it over them; the little crabs could no longer stare impudently up at them; their humiliating dependence upon the languid citizens of Obydos was at an end.

"In a week from now," observed Lady Oswestry, "we shall be at New York. Or we might," she added reflectively, "we might go direct to Southampton by way of Madeira. What do you say, Harry? Wouldn't that be possible?"

"Why, of course it would!" was the cheerful reply. "We can do whichever you like. Shall it be put to the vote?"

Southampton! New York! These words started a hundred different trains of thought. A very few hours ago Lady Oswestry's guests had despairingly regarded themselves as settled upon the Amazon bank hardly less permanently than the little crabs; now they felt they were as good as in London again. While the green wall of trees slipped monotonously before their eyes, it was not the forest which they saw but the shop-fronts of Piccadilly. And life forthwith quickened its rhythm; the talk at lunch turned upon old friends and new dresses. The desire for change, the thirst for distraction, became imperious. The quickest way home was voted the best.

Amongst the few who did not share in the general excitement was the professor. During the *Clio's* detention his equanimity had remained unshaken; the discovery of some interesting beetles in the mud bank had kept him more than content. His present intention was to disembark at Santarem and there await the next river steamer to Manaos. He took no account of the revolution. Nor did he care whether his steamer arrived in a few days, in a few weeks, or in a few months. In the mud of the Tapajos there was, no doubt, an equally fine assortment of coleoptera.

"We shall get to Santarem in another couple of hours," said Harry. "And Para we ought to reach some time to-morrow evening. The good old *Clio* is slipping along at a tremendous pace; the current, you must remember, is now with us."

Mr. Wilkinson had come to the decision to abandon his trip to Manaos. As he was taking coffee on deck he said to Harry: " My idea now is to proceed to Rio. If you will be so kind as to drop me at Para, I'll wait there for——"

" Humph ! " interjected Harry. " I think I should get out at Santarem, if I were you."

" Oh ! " And Mr. Wilkinson, slightly taken aback, fingered his chin.

Harry glanced round to see if they were being overheard.

" In strict confidence. . . ."

Mr. Wilkinson nodded wonderingly.

" We may not stop at Para at all."

" Oh ! " said Mr. Wilkinson again, and looked thoughtful. He knew that the others were all taking it for granted that a stop would be made at Para.

" We may find it—er—simpler to slip by in the night," said Harry.

And Mr. Wilkinson said no more.

The halt off Santarem was brief. Farewell shouts and fluttering handkerchiefs sped the professor and his companion on their way by boat to the landing-stage. At the same time the departing guests became the subject of varied discussion. Nearly everyone liked the professor, although it was agreed that to become well acquainted with him was an impossibility. " No one could have a more charming nature," said Lady Oswestry. " But his outlook is dreadfully limited; he takes positively no interest in human beings."

That, on the whole, the doctor considered, was

a rather refreshing trait. *His* complaint was that the professor thought too little about himself. It prevented him from developing an inner life. " I like egoists," he concluded, his eyes twinkling.

" Mr. Wilkinson, on the other hand, has plenty of inner life," observed Hugo meditatively.

The doctor smiled sardonically. " There are egoists and egoists," said he.

" I found Mr. Wilkinson a little dry," remarked Lady Oswestry. "·It is odd, but altruists generally are dry. Perhaps working for the good of humanity has a parching effect."

" Or perhaps those who erect love into a principle are precisely those who don't love by instinct. The professor, who only thinks about beetles, certainly has a much friendlier soul than Mr. Wilkinson."

It was the doctor who said this, and his remark was addressed to Hugo, for Lady Oswestry had already drifted away. Hugo's eyes were directed upon a sailor who was coiling a heavy rope on the lower deck.

" Mr. Wilkinson's mind," said he meditatively, " is dry, as you say ; but full—like a puff-ball. The mind of that man down there is empty, I suppose, in comparison ; but it contains a few hard, knobbly bits of practical experience. . . ."

" Which," added the doctor, " like the stones in the stomach of an ostrich, are useful aids to digestion."

Hugo remained silent for a time ; he was following his own thoughts ; at last with a sigh he said :

" Angela has no views on Mr. Bertrand Russell's

philosophy, but then on the subject of cami-knickers
Mr. Wilkinson's mind is quite equally blank."

"And on the Day of Judgment," said the doctor,
"when the secrets of the Universe become known,
I shan't be surprised to find that Angela has the laugh
on Mr. Wilkinson."

Hugo said no more. He was thinking that what
really mattered was the emotional intensity with
which one lived. Mary seemed to him to be much
more alive than anyone else on board. Besides—
and this was perhaps equally important—she had
l'âme bien née.

Words, gestures, and aspects of Mary which he
had hardly noticed at the time, now cropped up in
his memory. She was not particularly clever, her
tastes were not highly cultivated; but she was never
silly, never crude, never affected. Was it really
possible that she was still pledged to Gerald by feeling
as well as by word? He couldn't believe it. And
yet what evidence had he to the contrary? Hopes,
doubts, fears, chased one another tumultuously over
his heart; Mary was a tremendous excitement and a
tremendous mystery. She filled his whole being; he
was in love.

Never had he been in love with Stella. That was
now perfectly plain. He surveyed the liaison with a
certain distaste; unredeemed by any veritable
emotion did it now appear. In those days he had
been unfastidious simply because he had not been
in love. He had not known what it was to quiver
at the sound of a footstep, nor to ponder interminably
over the meaning of a look, a gesture, or an intonation,
—not to exist, in short, as anything more than a

shrinking, tremulous sensibility. New was the experience of having fallen out of the company of normal men, of having lost the good thick skin, the work-a-day sanity, the robust independence, of those who do not love. How he envied—and despised—those others! And how was he ever to be happy again, unless, by some miracle, Mary were to become afflicted with an answering madness?

The doctor left Hugo leaning over the rail, entirely absorbed by his thoughts. All the others, excepting Olga, had gone below for their siesta. Olga gazed on Hugo's clear-cut profile, and turned restlessly in her chair. During the last week she had been indulging in the fiction that he loved her. In the beginning she had fully realised that she was imposing upon herself; but she had yielded, yielded to the temptation to fill those days of tedium and discomfort with the enchanting imagery of dreams.

Rising from her place, she took a step towards the unconscious Hugo. The young man turned his head and stared, but without seeing her. Looking into his vacant eyes she stopped short, stood still for a moment, then wheeled despairingly round and disappeared down the companion-way; all this without his having become properly aware of her presence. She went to her cabin, took off her dress, threw herself upon her bed, and watched a lizard making short runs across the ceiling. Her cheeks burned; the blood throbbed in her temples; her heart was black with misery.

She was still lying in the same position when her maid entered and hung about the room, ostensibly to tidy up. Olga felt inclined to scream at her; but she set her jaw. She was fighting against a breakdown; to appear at dinner with red eyes—no, never! And Macpherson's presence acted as a restraint.

After a minute, however, a most unexpected thing happened. Without a sign of warning the impassive Scotchwoman threw up her hands and burst into loud hysterical weeping. Olga sat up and stared aghast. Then, before she had recovered herself or found a word to say, there came a knock at the door. At the same time it was half opened, and she heard Harry's voice asking if he might come in.

"No . . . yes . . . no," she replied.

Harry came in. He smiled at her reassuringly, gave Macpherson a scowl that partially silenced her, and said with an air of sublime competence:

"It's all right. I've just come for a chat." Then pointing at the maid. "I can explain those tears. Send her away for ten minutes, will you? And tell her that if she goes on blabbing I shall certainly hear of it, and ring her neck."

Olga was shaken out of herself. Feeling completely bewildered, she gave Macpherson a sign to retire. At the same time becoming aware of her disrobed condition, she slipped herself hastily under the sheet.

"I'll sit down, if you don't mind," said Harry, and he sat down. "I can't tell you how sorry I am to be bothering you, but that woman with her infernal love affair is getting us all into difficulties."

Olga gasped. "Love affair? Macpherson hasn't got a love affair."

"Oh, hasn't she!"

"Macpherson! She's not that kind. Besides, she's about forty and positively ugly."

"Not at all! She has her attractions," replied Harry.

"But how on earth should her love affairs. . . ."

Harry sighed profoundly and patted his forehead with a silk handkerchief.

"You look charming in bed," he threw out with a broad smirk.

Olga, who was recovering herself, assumed an expression of polite weariness. "Suppose we stick to Macpherson."

"She's a bit bony perhaps," said Harry judicially. "But she's tall, trim, and holds herself well. Besides, mark you! she's fair. And that in a country of dark, flabby women. . . ."

"But who? . . . But how has she got us into difficulties?"

"It's like this. She's hooked a wealthy storekeeper in Para, a Portuguese, forty-five, portly, respectable, plenty of money—a good match."

"How absurd!" exclaimed Olga.

"Not at all. She and her gent are in love."

Olga considered. If they were in love. . . .

"Well! what has it got to do with you?" she asked not without a touch of resentment.

"She's been bribing one of the crew to send and receive wireless messages. Her lover happens to possess a private set of his own."

"I thought our wireless was out of order."

Harry passed a hand over the mirror-like surface of his black hair. "Well, it isn't. I gave out that it was, because I didn't want it used. That's all."

"Why didn't you want it used?"

"Because it was better that the *Clio* should lie low. . . . I didn't want her whereabouts to be generally known in Para. . . . You see, I have had to consider the possibility of a counter-revolution there."

Olga was silent. She was thinking.

"God knows what that woman hasn't been saying over the wireless," Harry continued, grumbling. "And how can I tell whether her messages to her lover haven't been picked up by other stations in Para?"

Olga laughed, but her laugh was the cloak of an inward agitation. Macpherson had a lover! All the women in the world seemed to have lovers excepting herself. Harry, who had once paid her attentions was now turning to Stella. She felt resentful, and said:

"Poor Harry! It would be too bad if your wonderful revolution were to be spoilt by my maid, wouldn't it?"

Harry scowled. "The revolution won't suffer; *we'll* be the ones to suffer if——"

"If there *has* been a counter-revolution. And judging from your expression I should say there has. Well, you ought to have managed things better." And Olga smiled mockingly.

"Macpherson has been gossiping as well," Harry went on after a pause. "She has spread it about that the Federal party has regained power at Para and that we shall be detained."

"Well, she's right, isn't she?" inquired Olga flippantly.

"I don't know," Harry replied with deliberation. "I can't get Para to answer me at all. Something has happened, but what I don't know."

Olga shrugged. She had the air of enjoying herself. "Anyhow, you're responsible," she threw out.

Harry stared at her with heavy displeasure. "I shall kiss you in a minute," he returned at last, "but wholly and solely in order to annoy."

Olga made no answer.

"Once, I remember," Harry went on, "I made love to you. But since then I've discovered that I'm not made for love. I shall never marry."

Olga began to feel slightly embarrassed. "That's very interesting. But hadn't we better return to Macpherson? What do you want me to say to her?"

"You can tell her that we are going to try to slip past Para by night, unobserved. If she wants to join her man, I am willing to drop her in a small boat off the town. She can row herself in and take her chance."

"In that case I shall be left without a maid," observed Olga weakly.

Harry meditated. "I don't want to land her at Breves. That would be tantamount to giving notice of our approach. My idea is to make a straight bolt for the Atlantic."

"You are abandoning your new Brazilian friends, then?"

For a moment there was no reply, then Harry said: "I have my duty to you all."

Olga looked at him keenly. He shot his cuffs and fanned himself lazily with his handkerchief. He was impenetrable.

After a minute he got up. "You are ready to let Macpherson go? You must explain to her that she'll be taking risks: first, revolution and riot; secondly, a man who may be a scoundrel; thirdly, the climate. Are you inclined to dissuade her?"

"No!" replied Olga carelessly, although she coloured as she spoke. "Oh no!"

Harry laughed approvingly.

"Well . . . I must be off."

In the passage outside he was encountered by the doctor. They exchanged a meaning smile, and Harry followed him into his consulting room.

Olga looked up at the ceiling. The lizard was still there, but he seemed to have gone to sleep. She wished she could go to sleep—or die. Her heart was beginning to ache again.

She remained in her cabin for the rest of the day, alleging a headache. And the next morning it was the same: she could not bring herself to get up and appear on deck. It was the hottest day they had yet experienced. The *Clio* was engaged in re-threading her way through the narrow, airless channels connecting the Amazon with the Para estuary. Olga lay on her bed, loathing the clammy heat and fighting against a hatred of life.

Before lunch Stella and Mary came in to pay her a visit. Both had heard the rumour of a counter-revolution at Para; both were full of a suppressed excitement. Would the *Clio* be stopped and searched? Would they all be taken on shore and thrown into prison?

"What has Marion got to say about it?" asked Olga.

"She's not bothering," Mary replied in a low voice. "She's feeling too sad."

"One can hardly believe it," Mary continued after a silence, "but Harry says we shall reach Para this evening after dark, and to-morrow morning, if all goes well, we shall wake up in the Atlantic."

To each of them it seemed an age since she had felt the sea-breeze on her cheeks and smelt the smell of the brine. Immersed more profoundly than ever in the heavy, sticky heat, penetrated through and through by the languor of the tropics, they looked forward with eagerness to the renewal of their freshness and energy. Imaginatively they plunged into the world that to them was the real world, the world of grey skies, tumbling seas, fogs, frosts, warm clothes, and physical vigour. Actually they were still in an unreal world, a hothouse world, where the steamy atmosphere, the rich scents, and the unfamiliar vegetation, all seemed elements in a gigantic artifice. Never had this experience seemed more factitious than now, when it was within a few hours of becoming a memory.

It frightened Mary to reflect that Hugo had only revealed himself to her in this dream-life. Would he still be hers in London? Guiltily she thought: "Gerald has become illusory to me. Is it to be my punishment that I shall become illusory to Hugo?" In her panic she longed to go and fling her arms round his neck and implore him never, never to become a stranger to her. "You need not marry me," she would say; "I ask nothing of you except that you will remain the same—just the same, the Hugo whom I met in the forest and could not but love."

She did not know, as she looked out of the porthole and saw the green bank slipping by—she did not know that Hugo on deck was tormented with similar misgivings. "She only cared about me *out there*—and then it was chiefly pity. On the high seas, when her face is once again rosy from the wind, when she is once again wearing that little fur-trimmed coat of hers—ah, then it won't be of me but of Gerald that she will be thinking."

Chapter 21

PRESENTLY Mary rose and slipped away. After she had gone Stella, who was reclining in the arm-chair, continued to stare straight before her in silence, while Olga continued to look up at the ceiling.

"I should be amused," remarked Stella at last, "if we *were* all arrested at Para."

A bitter smile appeared on Olga's face. "Don't you want to get home?" she asked.

Something in her tone kept Stella silent for a moment. "I have no home to go to," she finally made answer.

"Ah!" And Olga gave a brief laugh.

"She means: 'You are lucky!'" said Stella to herself. "She means: 'I am one of the eighty per cent. who are sick of home; fed up with mama (probably with every justification); impatient, but unable, to marry; and incapable of leading an independent life.'"

After a pause Stella said: "My chief trouble is that I have very little money."

Olga gave the same bitter laugh. "I have plenty of money. What would *you* do if you had money?"

Then, as Stella seemed to have no answer ready, she went on: "What *shall* you do, anyhow?"

"Oh, I shall knock about by myself on the Continent. I shall write articles on political and economic conditions, on pictures, on books, on anything . . . I shall sit in cafés with Bohemians and Communists, and enjoy life."

" I wish I had your tastes as well as your abilities," said Olga.

" I know you," thought Stella. " From eighteen to twenty-two you were gaily prepared to admit that marriage was your intention, although in point of fact you were not thinking much about it. Since then you have become increasingly impatient to marry and proportionately less ready to confess even to yourself that marriage is desirable. Although normally and properly romantic, you are now more than prepared to marry any ' nice ' man who will do you credit. You would like your husband to be a gentleman, simple-minded, and constant in his affections —a man with a taste for family life, farming, and outdoor sport. You want to have children, to live in the country, to do just a little entertaining, and rarely—only very rarely—to visit London. The possibility that you may not realise your ambition gives you a grievance, a very serious grievance, against society. You know it, but you will not say it, nor do you even care to think it. You suffer under one the grossest mismanagements of civilisation —in a cowardly fashion—but with dignity."

These reflections aroused all Stella's exasperated sympathy for her own sex. She was a feminist who raged against the stupidity of women. She could not forbear to reply :

" Think of all the nice parties before you! The season is coming on. You and Angela will be having a perfect time, whilst I very likely shall not even manage to get abroad, but be obliged to remain scribbling in my sordid attic."

Olga was silent; and Stella continued her inward soliloquy: "Is it our own fault that our lives are more tragic than men's? Look at Marion Oswestry! She has had love, marriage, and children. Yet consider her now—with a withering skin, a useless arsenal of cosmetics, and the last of her love affairs behind her! Why is it that women who stand closer to nature, nevertheless prefer to take life secondhand—through men? Would Marion have been happier studying higher mathematics or working for the poor? I doubt it. She has lived the life that she was intended for."

In the meantime Olga had stretched out lazily to take a cigarette. Stella's last words were rankling in her mind. She half understood and half resented the feeling that prompted them.

"Parties bore one after a time," she observed. "Not that I don't enjoy seeing my friends as much as anyone. But it must be *so nice* to have an occupation. Writing, for instance, would be delightful to fall back upon." Her tone was just right; it put the proper distance between them again.

Stella's blue eyes became glassy from annoyance. Without another word she rose. But Olga went on talking, and had triumphantly reasserted herself before Stella managed to get out of the room.

All day there was an undercurrent of excitement on board. It was now generally known that if the *Clio* did stop at Para, her halt would not be a voluntary one. But why, somebody was inspired to ask, why

should she go near Para at all ? The full width of
the estuary was at least twelve miles. Did the shoals
outside the Ilha de Onças really constitute a serious
obstacle ? Well! someone else replied, what about
those despatches that Harry was pledged to deliver ?
Besides, was there any solid ground for believing
that Para had turned anti-revolutionary ? And would
it be generally known in Para that Harry was implicated in the revolution ?

At sunset the *Clio* was not far from Breves. Black
and deep was the *furo* along which she glided ; dense
and sheer were the walls of vegetation towering up
on either side. Dusk lay over the earth, but the sky
above was luminous and pink. The scene irresistibly
evoked memories of the outward journey. The pink
of the sky was the same. The glassiness of the water
was the same ; there was the same silence—a *positive*
silence that engulfed any sound that tried to break it.
The *Clio* moved like a ghost, and her company,
leaning in couples or singly over the rail, had the
sense of re-living insubstantially an hour that belonged
to the past. Speculation, so active all day, had
finished by burning itself out. The hot steamy
wilderness through which the *Clio* was meandering
appeared to be limitless in space as well as unchanging
in time. It became difficult to imagine an emergence
into other conditions. Never had the freedom and
stir of the Atlantic seemed more remote.

As the dusk thickened the human forms on deck
grew indistinct. Talk died down into fragmentary
murmurs, and then ceased altogether. In the distance
the lights of Breves were beginning to twinkle faintly.
The *Clio's* deck remained unlit ; spectre-like, the

ship glided along through a darkness that pressed close up against her.

So dark was it that Harry, standing in the bows, gave a start upon noticing that someone had approached him. It was his mother; she was leaning against the rail; her eyes seemed to be fixed upon the distant lights. After a while, without turning her head, she asked him at what hour they were likely to reach Para.

Her voice, which was very low, had a curiously dry quality. It was this, perhaps, which caused him to pause for an instant before replying: "Soon after midnight."

"Soon after midnight," she repeated in the same accents, and added: "Well! Have you nothing more to say to me?"

"Yes!" replied Harry. But after forcing out the word he remained without further speech.

She waited.

Harry drew himself up. At last he brought out: "I have spoken to McLaren. I told him—to prepare you . . . I said . . ."

"I want you to speak for yourself." She gave a little laugh. "Are you afraid of me, Harry?"

"Yes. I am." His tone was sullen.

She said, after a pause, very quietly: "You know I love you more than anyone on earth."

He gave a groan which was accompanied by a gesture of impatience. "All right," he replied with a kind of brutality. "I know that."

"You must explain——"

"I can't explain myself. Certainly not to you."

It was too dark to read his expression; but she could hear him breathing heavily.

Inexorable, she went on: "The moment has come when you really cannot refuse to speak to me—can you?" Her voice was calmer than ever. She even appeared to enjoy harrying him.

The pause that followed seemed endless. But at last—"My God!" Harry groaned, "I'm not like Hugo. I'm not civilised."

"What are you?"

"What?" One could fancy him to be grinding his teeth. "A buffoon! A comedian!" And he added morosely, viciously: "I tell you, I intend to have a run for my money!"

"But——"

"Leave me alone!" cried out Harry distractedly.

"In the past—have I ever stood in your way?"

He was silent.

"Have I ever thwarted you?"

"Leave me alone!" he cried again, making a gesture as if to sweep her right out of his sight. "You have had everything in life . . . you——"

"I had better die?"

"You must resign yourself."

In silence Lady Oswestry looked away. Although she still held herself as erect as ever, all the life seemed to have gone out of her. When she spoke again it was in a dull murmur. "I have lost James. I have grown old. And now——"

Harry stood stock-still and was voiceless for at least a minute, then abruptly: "Do you want me to blow my brains out?" he said.

"Oh, my darling!" His mother suddenly wrung

her hands. "In God's name, what is the matter with you? Why, why, why——"

"I tell you," said Harry, choking, "I would rather blow my brains out than go back to the old life."

She was silent.

"For years I've struggled to run away. You know it."

He waited in vain for a reply.

"Well! What do you want?" he continued in a kind of frenzy. "Am I to spend the rest of my days walking up and down St. James's Street? I can't do it. I don't justify myself. I won't do it."

"But——"

"Oh, yes!" he sneered, "now we shall have all the old arguments! Why don't I take a hand in something? Why not the House of Lords, committee meetings, public dinners? . . . Well, I can't —and I won't! That life is not for me. I have tried, and it's no use. I begin playing the fool. I'm not civilised, I tell you! If this little show fizzles out, I'll have a shot at the same thing somewhere else. Damn it! You don't take me for an Arthur Balfour, do you? I'm not even a Lloyd George or a Winston Churchill. I'm more like a little d'Annunzio, a *cabotin*, a comedian, a mountebank! But, unfortunately, without enough cant for the European stage. No! King of the Hottentots or Emperor of the Esquimaux is about my mark."

His mother stood facing him with rigidity. "All that is weakness," she pronounced in a flat voice.

Instead of answering Harry regarded her with a fixed gaze, then gave a brief laugh and allowed his arms to drop to his sides.

"If you like!" he muttered with indifference.

There was an interval during which they seemed to be eyeing one another coldly. At last, a sob bursting from her, she stepped forward and clutched him to her breast.

"Oh, Harry, I love you!"

"Don't! Don't!" he cried. And yet his arms gripped her with passion. "Mother, I implore you——"

"You do love me, Harry?"

"I do."

They stood there in close embrace—weak as water at first, but gradually, as their wills reasserted themselves, a stiffness crept over them. While the embrace still continued her pertinacity wrestled with his stubbornness. At her first involuntary stir he made haste to release her. They stood apart.

What next? the silence asked of them. What next? What next? His eyes travelled along the dark and now deserted deck. In a forced voice he observed:

"The others, I suppose, are at dinner."

She received this with a little sound that was like a sneer. "In a few hours"—she stated it coldly—"you leave me!"

"Yes."

She repeated the sound. She drummed with her fingers upon the wood of the rail.

At last—"Harry——!" she began, and then incontinently stopped. It was as if she had been able—in spite of the darkness—to perceive his singular grimace.

The seconds went by. Not a sign came from

either of them. Lady Oswestry's lips were parted. Surely there must exist some word, some cry, some magic syllables, that would avert the catastrophe? She stood with eyes fixed and limbs rigid. The hot damp air brushed past her; the murmur of the engines filled her ears; she was going down, down, into the gulf of her despair.

At last she stirred slowly into motion. Slowly she walked away. Her son's eyes followed her figure for as far as possible along the obscure deck; she was quite lost to sight before she reached the companion-way.

Chapter 22

IN the meantime the lights of Breves had shifted round to the stern. The *Clio* had emerged from the last of the *furos* and was now driving at full-speed through the broad waters of the Bay of Marajo. Harry turned, stared into the unrelieved darkness ahead, and drew a deep breath.

Some minutes elapsed before he went below. In his cabin he tossed off a tumbler of cold water, mopped his brow, and scrutinised himself closely in the mirror. His hair, he found, was slightly ruffled. A few strokes of the brush were necessary to restore it to its glass-like smoothness. After this he sat down and whistled softly to himself.

His next move was to press the bell-button, and on the appearance of his manservant he ordered some sandwiches and a whisky and soda. Gradually, as he munched his sandwiches and watched the man packing his clothes, a look of content spread over his face.

"Mrs. Barlow is in at dinner, I suppose?"

"Yes, m'lord."

Harry considered. "Well, go and tell Mrs. Barlow that her ladyship would like to speak to her. Then bring Mrs. Barlow to me. I shall be on deck."

With a cigarette between his lips he mounted the

companion-way and waited. In a few minutes a
broad beam of light cut the darkness. The saloon
door had opened, Stella was coming out. He stepped
out of the obscurity, causing her to give a start.
She said:

"Hullo! I'm told your mother wants me."

"*I* want you," he replied; and his hand upon
her arm invited her to accompany him along the
deck. In silence they went forward to the bows.
"In sending for you just now," he explained with
elaboration, "a strict regard for the conventions
prompted me to substitute my mother's name for
mine."

"I see," said Stella.

Although the night was becoming suffused with
starlight he could not tell whether she was smiling
or grave.

"Perhaps," he went on after a moment, "perhaps
you have noticed that I have been rather reticent
during the last few days?"

"No! Have you?" answered Stella, who, as a
matter of fact, had been considerably piqued by his
aloofness.

Harry stroked his jaw. "Well! now the time has
come——" He hesitated, then broke off with an
upward lift of his head. "Excuse me! Did you
hear a booming just now— a low distant booming?"

Stella looked up sharply.

"No . . ." And she listened. "No, I don't
think so."

"Humph!" And Harry again rubbed his blue-
black jaw. "Never mind. It may have been my
imagination." He paused. "I wanted to ask you,

have you read that little memorandum I gave you some days ago?"

"Yes," replied Stella slowly, "I have."

He waited.

"Really it seemed to me rather fantastic," she finally blurted out. "Are you serious in saying that you have a million pounds to play with? And are you really prepared to risk the whole of it here?"

Harry nodded. "Why not? The money's mine. I'm not robbing my mother or Hugo. That million represents my winnings—at the end of five years' gambling."

"But why hand it over to a mushroom Government?"

"I shan't hand it over exactly. I—well, I intend to administer the finances of this country myself."

"Oh!" ejaculated Stella significantly, and fell into the silence of meditation.

Harry cleared his throat and threw out a hand in true oratorical style. "My modest hope is that within the next few days I shall have constituted myself the virtual dictator of Amazonia. My friend, Pedro Andrade, is going to be the figure-head, but mine will be the power behind the throne. I need hardly inform you that the Federal Government at Rio would sacrifice a great deal for the sake of ready money. I shall be in a strong position to negotiate. A million sterling at the present rate of exchange represents quite a respectable sum in Brazil; and then of course there is the great wealth behind the Andrades. Can you doubt that I am the man to handle this situation? No! And putting the money question aside, my qualifications must, I should think, be obvious—even to the intelligence of a Brazilian."

Stella's face was upturned. It might have been an effect of the starlight, but her eyes seemed to sparkle.

"Well," continued Harry in his lordliest manner, "this being the position, I offer you—oh, damn!"

She was bewildered. He was not looking at her any longer; he was staring hard just over her shoulder. She wheeled round. What on earth had he found to be gazing at? Then she saw a strong red glow on the horizon.

"Is it . . ." she stammered, "can it be the lights of Para?"

Harry was scowling heavily. "It's either that—or else Para is burning."

A silence followed. Both were gazing with intentness into the dark. At last, faintly smiling, Stella shot a glance at her companion. He looked big and sulky. She could hear him cursing beneath his breath.

All at once he spun round. "Hi, there!" he shouted. "Stanford!"

In a few seconds the young man came hurrying up. Harry pointed to the distant glow. "What's that? What has Joao got to say about it? Go and ask him."

The answer was prompt. "Joao has just this moment told me that on some nights you get a much bigger glow from the town than you would expect."

Harry passed a hand over his sleek hair and heaved a sigh.

"That's good," he replied at last. "Got anything else to report?"

"No, sir—messages are all being jammed."

Harry grunted and fell into meditation. He continued to meditate for some while after Stanford had withdrawn.

Finally Stella made a movement of impatience. "I think Hugh Stanford has recovered from his love for Mary," she observed.

"Nothing like science to cure you of love," answered Harry, coming out of his muse. And then: "Am I to encourage science in Amazonia?" he asked suddenly.

"Yes, of course."

"All right. But what about art and literature? I've no use for them myself."

Stella frowned. "Go for material prosperity—and the rest shall be added unto you—perhaps. But you speak as if you were going to spend the remainder of your life out here."

"I shall stay unless I get chivied out of the country—or murdered."

Stella gave a little laugh. "I think you exaggerate."

"The risks? Perhaps. But I feel bound to put them before you."

"Oh! Why?"

She had the courage to add the Why, because the others, having finished their dinner, were trooping along the deck and there was no time for Harry to answer. One and all they betrayed, in their different fashions, the excitement that possessed them. Olga was loquacious in her most nonchalant society manner. Francis, professing to be a little drunk, danced about the deck, chattering like a magpie; and Angela egged him on. Mary and Hugo seemed to be lost in a dream, but in a dream of greater intensity than any waking experience.

To Stella's sense those two spread an extraordinary atmosphere of romance about them. They made vivid the stillness and starriness of the night. She became aware of the huge, warm solitude through which the *Clio* was speeding, and the ship's onward rush seemed significant; it was as though she were flying from something, or seeking something, with secret passion.

Harry's voice broke in upon her abstraction; the others had moved away; they were alone again. It was not without surprise that she took in the sense of his words. He had said: " Don't you envy Francis and Angela ? "

She considered. If he had said, " Don't you envy Hugo and Mary ? " she would have understood him better, although she would have felt slightly annoyed. Before she had found her reply, Harry went on in the voice of one making a quotation: " It is not sin but triviality that hideth us from God."

Stella frowned. This was not the Harry she knew. This was not the Harry of her imagination. She was tired of the religious sense in humankind.

" God doesn't bother *me!* " she returned dryly.

Harry laughed, or rather guffawed. It seemed as though he took the hint. At any rate, it was with all his old swagger that he next said:

" I intend to build a palace upon the island of

Marajo. There are magnificent sites upon the rocky eastern shore. My palace will front the Atlantic. Baroque style, I think. Eh?"

Stella answered with a laugh.

"By the way," continued Harry carelessly, "your husband has left this country."

"Oh!"

"So how would you like to stay here?"

"With you? Many thanks for the suggestion."

One way and another it would mean taking a good deal of risk."

"Oh, *that* I don't mind."

"Well, then?"

Stella was trembling slightly. She paused to steady her voice. "In the first place, I'm not sure—although you seem to take it very much for granted—that I care to become your mistress."

Harry shifted from one foot to another. And as Stella looked at him she realised that he had been seized with confusion.

"No! Quite so!" he stammered. "Of course not. In fact, I myself——"

"Oh!" cried Stella, furious. "I see! You want me just as a companion? A lady-help? Is that it?"

Harry gave a sigh of relief. "Please! Please don't put it like that! Let us rather look upon the arrangement——"

"I like your insolence," interrupted Stella, laughing through her mortification. "You ask me to throw away my reputation and run the risks of malaria, murder, and sudden death, just for the pleasure of your charming conversation. Perhaps your idea is that I should be housekeeper for your Brazilian harem?"

"My dear child!" cried Harry, seizing her by the arm. "Listen before you go on! What I want"—and he paused impressively—"is to make you Empress of Amazonia!"

"My dear man," returned Stella with false calm, "I'm afraid you really are a little insane."

Harry shook her arm impatiently. "Be quiet and listen! This is no sudden freak of mine. I have made a study of you."

Stella contented herself with a sigh and a shrug.

"You are a very sensible young woman of a strong, independent character—and healthy tastes."

"Thank you."

"For instance, you have a taste for good-looking young men. Your husband was a handsome man. . . . And then Hugo——"

"That will do!" snapped out Stella.

"Well"—and Harry held up a finger to give emphasis to his next words—"I ask you, have you ever seen a more charming, a more beautiful creature than young Pedro Andrade?"

Stella stood still, dumbfounded, and the expression of outrage on her face gradually gave place to one of awe. Her memory took her back to the night when Pedro had boarded the *Clio* . . . ! She bethought her of Harry with his electric torch . . . ! Was it possible . . . ? Had he already supposed . . . ? Good God! What a man! What a monster!

In a daze she listened to Harry expounding his scheme. And how she detested his persuasiveness, his heavy jauntiness! She was not really in love with him, but . . . Idiot! He was telling her that he had "made a study" of Pedro and was convinced

that the young man would be "bowled over" by
her. She must remember her blue eyes and fair
hair. . . . Undoubtedly they would "do the trick."
As for her other qualifications, she had, without
question, a stronger character than Pedro's. He
would count on her to keep Pedro out of mischief
and to consolidate his own influence over him. He was
sure—oh, absolutely sure!—that not only would Pedro
become her slave, but that in a short time *she* would
become devoted to *him ;* for dear Pedro was one of the
best—as white as they made 'em, in spite of being a
Dago. He hoped she wouldn't mind having children by
him? Rather amusing to start a new dynasty, eh?

Stella was saved from the necessity of answering
by a sudden interruption. Captain Wilson, who was
now almost himself again, had come up, accompanied
by the first officer, the chief engineer, and Mr. Simpson.
These men in a body made a determined call upon
Harry's attention. The latter grumbled, but was
prevailed upon to move to the door of the wheel-
house where they all stood in earnest conference.
A few minutes later the *Clio's* speed was reduced to
dead-slow. Joao's voice, raised in excitement, could
be heard all over the ship.

Twenty minutes went by before a conclusion was
reached. The group dispersed. Joao, apparently
appeased, rejoined Joachim at the wheel, and once
more the *Clio* was urged full-speed ahead. She was
now entering the channel between the Isla de Onças
and the mainland. The glow in the sky marking
the position of Para was becoming every instant
more bright. Light-buoys indicated the fairway.
One had the sense of drawing near to civilisation again.

None of the passengers, however, was quite prepared for the sudden change that awaited them upon rounding the next bend. All in one moment the water-front of Para came into full view, and the reach in between was crowded, or so it seemed, with shipping. The *Clio* was steering a course that would carry her past the town without going any nearer to it than was necessary. Everyone crowded to the starboard rail and gazed at the lights hung in random fashion upon the black curtain of the night. There were red lights and green lights, lights fixed and lights moving, electric signs, shifting patterns of light; and this illumination quivered in long streamers across the dark water; like paper carnival ribbons they stretched right up to the *Clio* herself.

The plunge from the wilderness into the society of man produced an effervescence of excitement on board. It was thrilling to hear the whistles of steam-craft, the rattle of chains, distant hails, and the far-away but substantial rumour of the town. What of the forest now? Amazonia's austere figure of savagery had been miraculously trivialised. Here was her darkness tricked out with spangles; the fussy noises of an alien life made light of her immemorial silences.

But, although elated, the travellers on the *Clio* could not forget that their companionable sentiments might not be reciprocated. If something outside the ordinary was going on, weren't they implicated? And something extraordinary *was* going on. Not without disquiet did they observe a rusty haze of smoke hanging over one quarter of the town. In

Stella this portent aroused a feeling of positive dismay.
Poor Harry!

As she was murmuring this to herself, a spurt of angry flame went up into the sky.

"A roof falling in!" she could not but cry out.

"Yes. But nothing of importance!"

It was Harry's voice. He had just come up behind her. "Filthy district, that! I shall rebuild it on modern lines."

So saying, he drew her away from the others. She followed, unresisting, but not for more than a few steps. A new sound from over the water brought her to a startled halt. Unmistakably it was the crackle of a fusillade.

All conversation on the deck dropped in an instant. And then the whole night seemed to fill with a low deep vibration, a noise more prolonged and menacing than the roar of any beast, the voice of an angry mob.

"Your welcome, Harry!"

These words came from Lady Oswestry, whose figure emerged unexpectedly out of the dark. Neither Harry nor Stella had known she was on deck. The quiet bitterness of her tone bespoke nothing but resignation.

Harry brought out a little laugh. "Oh, that's—that's only a trifle! If the trouble were serious the warships would be taking part."

Without saying anything more his mother moved away.

Looking round carefully to see that he could not be overheard, Harry turned to his companion.

"Well!" He was fixing her intently. "What do you think? Is it too much of a gamble?"

Stella stood very still.

"I feel sorry for your mother," she murmured.

"Yes. . . . Rough luck! Especially after old James's death." He stopped with a jerk.

Tense and painful was the silence that followed.

"Perhaps"—Harry evidently was speaking with the greatest effort—"perhaps you'd do better to keep out of it."

Stella seemed to gasp. "I don't know. I'm thinking . . . What would your mother say? And all the rest?"

Harry was evidently ready for this. "I should tell them that you were dutifully rejoining your husband. For all they know, he's still in Para."

Stella looked round helplessly, desperately. She could just make out the forms of the others, who were hanging with excitement across the rail. Beyond, over their shoulders, glittered the lights of Para. The *Clio* was gliding along the edge of the darkness—slinking, so it seemed to her, like a cat along the base of a wall. She noticed that the water-front of the town was shifting slowly to the rear. In a few minutes . . .

Quite suddenly she made a small, inarticulate sound, a sound scarcely audible yet absolutely decisive. At the same instant, too, with a jerk of the shoulders she moved in the direction of the companion-way.

"Damn it!" cried Harry, and he placed himself in front of her. "You've got to answer! And pretty quick. In less than——"

"Let me pass!" snapped out Stella. "I want to pack."

But Harry continued to obstruct her way. It was half a minute before he made any response.

Then: "Haw, haw!" he ejaculated in an extraordinary bray of satisfaction. And holding out his hand, "Put it there!" he said.

Stella put it there.

His face was beaming, he was full of chuckles, as he hurried off to the wheel-house; but on entering he became severely matter-of-fact.

"Well, skipper! We've done it, eh?"

"Seems so," admitted the captain.

"In another minute or two we'll stop to lower the boat."

The other said nothing; his looks were quite sufficiently eloquent.

In silence and with one accord the two men turned and gazed ahead. The *Clio's* bows were again pointing into darkness—a darkness relieved only by the light-buoys marking her channel down to the Atlantic.

Presently Harry gave a sign; the bell tinkled peremptorily; the engines stopped. After drifting forward for a minute, the *Clio* lay dead still upon the smooth, starry water.

"Well," said Francis to Angela in a tone of relief; "that's that!" And, beneath his breath he added: "At least as far as *we* are concerned."

Although coloured in each case by different shades of feeling, this reflection was shared by all the watchers on deck. In every mind, too, the memory of Sir James had suddenly become insistent. It was uncanny to think of him remaining behind there all alone. In that far place, underneath the howling monkeys, he was lodged to the end of time. Sir James! Who would have thought it!

Francis, however, did not linger upon that thought

for long. Nor was it long before his relief was tinctured by a certain sense of flatness. Here was the close of an episode which left his life absolutely unchanged. He was returning to an existence full of difficult expedients. No bank balance, a host of creditors, no settled occupation, no prospects, no purpose. But he faced the future with a cheerful, unthinking stoicism. He knew that thinking was no use.

As for Angela, she acknowledged Francis's observation with the faintest of shrugs. Upon her face there hovered a delicate, dreamy smile. Without a thought for the years when her beauty would have fled, she smiled—she smiled (unconscious ironist!) at these moments of the present, so heavy with emotions which she did not share.

Actually what amused her most was the news (just received) that Stella had decided to land at Para. She gave her reading of this information to Olga, in whose bosom it stuck like a small poisoned dart. Harry had preferred *Stella!* Yes! because *she* had the secret of coming to grips with life. *She* had pluck!

It did not occur to Olga that her own pluck, if different, was perhaps not less.

The only tears that were shed came from the eyes of Mary, in whom there was so deep a happiness that she could afford to weep. Hugo grieved, but not even his mother's anguish could distract him from the delicious agitation by which he was possessed. For he was still uncertain. His foolish heart still questioned: "Is my love returned?" Before him stretched an exquisite vista, full of mysteries and discoveries; ardent, he was waiting to be cured of his unbelief.

With an arm round his mother's shoulders he stood as still as she. Lady Oswestry had nothing more to do, nothing more to say. This unenjoyable interval was imposed by the last petty details of the departure. Stewards were hurrying about the deck with luggage; a boat was being lowered; it fell presently with a smack upon the water.

By an occasional pressure of his arm Hugo endeavoured to convey his sympathy. Inwardly he was railing at the delay. And all at once his silent curses redoubled in vigour. Out of the night came a crisp, dry rattling. Dimmed though it was by the distance, he could scarcely hope that his mother mistook the sound. It was the rattling of machine-guns.

Harry's voice rang out cheerfully. He was standing at the head of the ladder. " Now then, Macpherson ! Down you go ! "

The boat beneath was already heaped up with luggage. Stella had already chosen her seat in the bows. In another moment Harry, standing amidships, shoved off.

The company on the *Clio* hung over the rail in silence—in a silence which Harry had enjoined and which no one felt any impulse to break.

After the boat had drifted a few yards away, Harry signalled with his arm. Captain Wilson went at once to the wheel-house; the bell rang; the *Clio's* screw began to throw up a faintly phosphorescent foam.

For a minute the boat remained distinguishable as a darker blot upon the darkness. When it had quite disappeared, Lady Oswestry went below.

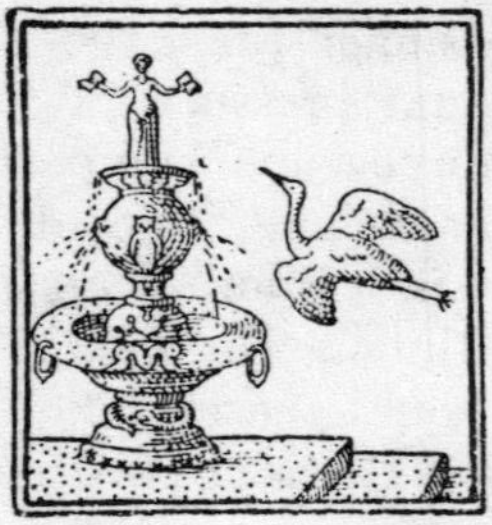